The Onion Caper

The man had his back to Cole, totally focused on kicking Jason. Cole sprinted on the balls of his feet. The guy looked up just as Cole drove a shoulder into his side, like blind-siding a quarterback. They both went down. Cole bounced up thinking the other guy would stay down. To his surprise the thug jumped up and squared off in a fighting stance.

They eyed each other a second, before the guy took a wild swing at Cole's head. Cole leaned back from the blow. He tried to see the face under the hoodie but the overhead light shone behind the stranger. Cole started to wade into the attacker when the guy reached in his pocket and pulled out a knife. The blade sprung from the handle. Cole stared at the weapon and stumbled back a few more paces. His own right hand dug into his pocket and closed on the lock-blade Buck. He pulled it out and fumbled to open the blade.

What am I doing? I can't get into a knife fight. I'll get killed. But he held it up for the other man to see. They circled each other. Cole's every nerve concentrated on his opponent. Fear gripped his stomach, as his brain screamed--Run! He skittered around defensively, trying to keep his distance from the attacker, and the silver blade he waved. Lurching to the side, Cole bumped into the dumpster and stumbled for balance.

An excruciating pain exploded in the back of his head. Next thing he knew he sprawled face down in the rubble. Multi-colored spots danced in his eyes. His brain refused to focus. Dizziness distorted everything. Shifting to his right side, he lifted a hand to the back of his head. It came away wet. Lying on the ground, Cole fought to remain conscious. He heard another voice behind him.

"Kill both the sons-a-bitches and let's get out of here."

Wings

THE ONION CAPER

William O. Weldy

A Wings ePress, Inc.

Young Adult Novel

Wings ePress, Inc.

Edited by: Leslie Hodges
Copy Edited by: Jeanne Smith
Senior Editor: Anita York
Executive Editor: Marilyn Kapp
Cover Artist: Pat Evans

All rights reserved

Wings ePress Books
http://www.wings-press.com

Copyright © 2013 by William O. Weldy
ISBN 978-1-61309-920-9

Published In the United States Of America

Wings ePress Inc.
3000 N. Rock Road
Newton, KS 67114

Dedication

For the old boys from the projects

One

Cole McKenna sat Indian style, hunched over his bicycle chain replacing a universal link. The afternoon sun baked his already tanned back. Sweat ran into his eyes. He wiped his forehead with the back of a grease-smudged hand. According to the TV weatherman, the summer of 1985 was the hottest on record for Ohio since the 1930's. Fitting the chain to the bike sprocket, Cole caught sight of Jack and Dale Shaw running across the common area toward him. .

Uh-oh. Here comes trouble. Mom didn't want him to hang out with the Shaw boys, but they were hard to avoid sometimes. Six brothers--all of them ill-tempered--made the Shaws a feared gang in the projects. The oldest brother, Chuck, had left in a rush last year and not returned. Gene, the next oldest, was serving time in reform school. That left Jack as the self-designated leader of the juveniles in the projects. Jack was pure-mean and Dale his back-up. Together they thrived on bullying the weaker kids. They threw rocks at chained up dogs, tormented stray cats, and stole anything not nailed down. Once Cole watched Jack saunter up to a group of young girls playing hop scotch. He had a dead cat draped around his neck like a scarf. Thinking it to be a pet, the girls ooohed and aaahed over the cute little kitty as Jack stroked it lovingly. When Jack swung the stiff carcass by the tail, and smashed it into a tree trunk, the girls shrieked in horror and ran for their homes. Jack laughed like a hyena.

"Hey, Cole, want to go to a movie with us?" Jack asked all friendly like.

"Can't," Cole said, "ain't got enough money."

"Get some from your mom," Dale said.

Cole concentrated on the chain. "I Can't, she's working."

"Back to the Future's playing," Jack teased.

Cole's interest piqued. Despite his reluctance to hang out with the Shaws, he really wanted to see that movie. "Man, I wish I could but..."

Jack dug his hand into his pocket and came up with some change. "How much money you got, Cole? Maybe I got a plan."

Cole hesitated, eying Jack, then said, "About a buck I guess. Not enough."

"Me and Dale got over a dollar between us. Maybe we could pool our money and buy a ticket."

Cole calculated in his head. The local theater cost two dollars. They didn't want him to go; they just wanted his money. Cole stood up in case this got ugly. "I don't think so, Jack."

"Now wait a minute," Jack started. "You don't understand. See we buy a ticket for one of us to go in and then when the lights dim, the one inside goes to that side exit door and opens it for the others to sneak in. We've done it before. It always works, don't it, Dale?"

"Sure." Dale Tucked his chin down and opened his hands as if it were a no-brainer.

Cole thought it over. He really wanted to see Back to the Future. His face pinched with indecision. "Nope. I can't," he finally said. "If they catch us, Mom will ground me for life."

"Oh, they won't catch us," Jack said. "But even if they do, they just throw us out. And they even give our money back. We've done it lots of times,"

Every thought in Cole's head told him to pass this up. He couldn't. He wanted to see that movie.

To his surprise, the ploy worked out just as Jack had described. So that hot August night, walking home from the movie, Cole's mind dwelled on possible time travel and cool cars. The trio had cut through yards and alleys on the way to the projects and Cole hadn't paid much attention. His thoughts jarred to the present when Jack jerked to a stop and said, "What in the hell is that?" pointing to a large glass structure attached to the back of a house.

Cole followed Jack's finger. His eyes squinted to focus in the dim street light. "Well," he said. "I think it's a greenhouse. My Grandma has a small one on her farm. But hers ain't attached to the house like this one. They start plants in the winter for early planting in the garden."

"Man, we need some rocks for this," Jack said with glee.

Instantly knowing where this was about to go, Cole said, "Wait, Jack. The noise will bring 'em running. Why don't we see what's in the garden first? Maybe there's watermelon."

"Yeah," Dale said. "I'm hungry."

Without giving Jack a chance to think about it, Cole vaulted over the picket fence and into the garden. The others followed. As Cole carefully trod between the rows of vegetables he cringed when Jack and Dale trampled the plants down. Grandma would tan their hides. They strolled through the garden, pulling carrots and onions and crunching others under foot. No watermelons could be found.

Jack pulled an onion from the ground and held it up. "Look at the size of these damn onions."

All the onion plants were huge with large flowering bulbs at the tops. Most couldn't even be pulled out of the ground without breaking the stems. Jack pulled or broke several trying to find small tender ones. After they had eaten a few smaller onions and carrots,

Cole noticed Jack apparently looking around for rocks. "Last one to Bolton's is queer," he called out, and started for the fence.

Bolton's, a small neighborhood grocery store, marked the entrance to the projects, where they all lived. Cole hated the projects. Living there labeled him poor white trash.

The boys jumped the fence and tore off laughing. Half a block from the store, Cole slowed a bit to allow Jack and Dale to pass him. He knew they didn't like to lose races.

"I guess that makes you queer, Cole," Jack taunted.

~ * ~

The next morning Cole's mother called to him from the kitchen door. "Cole Mckenna, get in here! There's a policeman here to see you. What in the hell have you done?"

Fear surged through Cole's mind as he frantically tried to think of why the cops would want him. Did they know about sneaking in the movie? No, it had to be the garden. "Nothing Mom, really," Cole called out defensively.

When Cole entered the small kitchen, the serious glare of the officer stopped him cold. The cop didn't look mad, but his steel gray eyes bore into Cole's soul.

Cole felt an immediate awe of the officer and at the same time a deadly fear. Before Cole's brain could clear, the officer said, "I understand you and the Shaw boys raided a garden last night."

"What?" his mother gasped, "Cole wouldn't..." Then, "Raiding a garden? My God. That's a petty thing."

"Yes, Ma'am," the officer said. But Cole and two of the Shaw boys did some damage to a garden on Ridge Avenue last night."

Cole's mind raced. How *could he have known it was us?* It had been dark. No lights in any of the houses. They'd only been there a few minutes. Cole had seen many cop shows on TV like Hill Street

Blues and Magnum PI. He knew they had sophisticated investigative techniques he didn't understand, but this went beyond his comprehension. His mind continued to race with thoughts of the how smart this policeman must be to have figured out the crime in such a short time. Cole's thoughts were so focused on the impressive image and obvious brilliance of the officer; he almost forgot why he was there.

"Well, Cole, what do you have to say for yourself?"

Cole's mind jerked back to his predicament but he couldn't think clearly--his mind jumbled with fear. Should he try to lie? But he could tell that the officer knew the truth. After a long pause, he managed, "But we only ate a few onions." By his frame of reference it couldn't be a big deal; kids have raided gardens since the beginning of time. Now he would be going to jail for something he didn't even think of as a crime.

"Those onions were seed onions Mr. Turner cultivated for sale and what you guys didn't pull up, you trampled down. So it's a little more serious that just eating a few onions." With that, the officer pulled a leather pad from his rear pocket and began writing.

Cole reached for his mother. "I don't want to go to jail, Mom," he wailed as he clung to her.

"Isn't there some other way we can handle this?" Cole's mother pleaded. "This seems so minor."

"I'm afraid not, Ma'am. Oh, he won't have to go to jail, but you and he will have to appear in Juvenile Court to answer to the crime. I think there's an important lesson to be learned here," he said, handing the slip of paper to Mrs. McKenna.

The officer looked at Cole. "You might want to consider not hanging around with those Shaw boys. Most of them already have juvenile records and it looks like they're not about to change."

"Oh, he won't be," his mother chimed in. "He's not supposed to play with those brats anyway." Cole's Mom gave him a hard glare. "They're foul-mouthed and mean."

Cole just hung his head in shame.

"Have Cole at the juvenile hearing on the date on the citation, Ma'am," the officer said as he turned for the door.

After the officer left, Cole's mind whirled with wonder about him. He'd never had direct contact with a police officer before. What would it be like to be a cop?

~ * ~

Two weeks later, Cole found himself staring in wonder at the massive domed ceiling of the county court house. He'd never been inside the building, although he had walked and ridden his bike past it many times. He and his mother trudged up the stairs to the third floor. The musty smell of the old building was somewhat masked by disinfectant. A large set of heavy wooden doors with the sign 'Juvenile Court' over the top told them they had arrived. They entered and were directed to take a seat in the front row.

After a short wait, a lady dressed in a blue suit jacket, a lacy white blouse and blue pants entered and sat behind a large desk. "Are you Cole McKenna?" she asked.

Dazed, Cole looked around the empty room then jolted back when he heard his name. His embarrassment rendered him mute until his mother elbowed him. "Yes, Ma'am," he muttered.

"I am Jennifer Sanders, the county juvenile probation officer and court referee. Do you understand why you are here, Mr. McKenna?"

"Yes, I guess so," Cole stammered, then added, "Ma'am."

"You've been charged with petit theft and destruction of property. How do you plead--guilty or not guilty?"

Cole's heart sank. He felt his body temperature soar. He looked to his mom. His mouth and face went slack. Those words sounded so serious. He'd never been so frightened. He forgot to breathe. Finally his mother nudged him and nodded toward the referee.

"Oh," he mumbled looking at his shoes. "Guilty, I guess." Immediately after uttering those words, he indeed felt guilty--guilty and so ashamed that he wanted to crawl under the bench seat and never come out. What the referee said after that, Cole had little recollection of.

Leaving the court house, Cole's mom pulled him along at a rapid pace; her heels stomped into the concrete. With every step he could see her anger building. "You, young man," she stopped and turned Cole, "are now grounded for the same three months as your probation. I mean it, Cole. Except for school you will be in the house every minute."

Cole said nothing. Whatever punishment his mother gave him couldn't compare to the mortification he felt from being labeled a criminal.

"That three dollar and fifty cent fine I paid is nothing compared to the day's pay I've lost from taking off work." She started off, dragging Cole, then stopped again. "Cole, we need every penny I make just to live. How could you?"

Cole saw tears welling in her eyes. "I'm so sorry, Mom."

She pulled him to her chest and squeezed him. "I know, Hon; it's just so hard..." They stood locked together crying.

Now Cole was officially a criminal. He burrowed deeper into himself feeling so alone. He was sure everyone at school would find out and shun him even further than he perceived they already did. No longer just poor white trash living in the projects with a drunken father who wouldn't work, now on top of his already embarrassing life--a criminal.

Two

Cole did his best to avoid the Shaw brothers during school days. He often stayed inside during recess to study. The Shaws didn't participate in school sports and Cole's time spent in after-school practices and doing homework kept him busy in the evenings. Weekends were more difficult, but being grounded helped.

Near the end of the school year Pickaway county officials announced there would be a track and field competition between small town elementary schools for the county championship. Cole struggled with indecision all that week. Should he enter? Brockton Elementary didn't have an official track team, but the boys often raced on the playground. Cole loved to compete but dreaded the attention of individual sports. He made his decision Friday, after Mr. Hormel, the school principal, called him to his office.

"Cole, I see you haven't signed up for the track meet qualifications yet. Why not?"

"I don't know," Cole said, looking down.

"Look, Cole," Mr. Hormel said, leaning forward in his chair. "By now I think I know you pretty well. I know you're shy but you're one of our best athletes, even when you don't try your hardest." He dropped his chin and looked at Cole over the rim of his glasses.

Cole knew Mr. Hormel had been a college jock by all the pictures on his wall and the general scuttle-butt around school. In addition to being principal in this small school, Mr. Hormel chose to be the coach for sports programs as well. Cole admired Mr. Hormel and didn't want to disappoint him.

"Cole this isn't just about you. It's about our school. Now I know you're a fast runner. Don't you want us to win the county championship?"

"Well, yeah, but..."

"No buts, Cole. We need you, okay?"

"Yeah, I guess so." Cole continued to stare at his knees.

"Okay then." Mr. Hormel smiled. "I've watched you on the basketball court and in gymnastics. I know you can jump. So in addition to the sprint I want you to enter the high jump and the long jump. Depending on how well you do in qualifications, you may be on the relay team as well."

Mr. Hormel slid the sign-up sheet and a pen toward Cole.

Cole printed his name under the events Mr. Hormel had directed and signed the bottom.

The student body was released to the playground for track qualifications that day. Even though he tried not to stand out during qualifications, Cole finished third in the Sprint. He would have had to stop to let the boy in fourth place pass him. Jack and Dale Shaw finished fifth and sixth. Cole finished first in both the high jump and long jump mainly because he had no idea how high or far the others could jump.

After school Jack Shaw sprang around the far corner of the building as Cole walked by and grabbed him in a headlock. Dale stood ready to help if Jack needed it. "How the hell did you beat me in that race?" Jack demanded. "You never have before. You know I'm faster than you."

"I don't know," Cole mumbled through Jack's arm. *I would have had to take a nap for you to catch up,* he thought.

"Well, you'd better drop out and let me run in that track meet or we'll beat your ass."

Cole struggled to free himself. "I didn't want to race anyway. Mr. Hormel made me."

Jack eased his hold on Cole's neck and Cole jerked his head free. He moved back a step and made ready for another attack. "You'd better drop out," Jack warned, pointing a rigid finger at Cole, as he and Dale swaggered away.

The rest of the day Cole thought about Jack's threats. He didn't want to fight both Jack and Dale, but... sooner or later he'd probably have to. He couldn't just ignore the bullying forever. *I'm not really afraid of him,* Cole thought. Up 'til now it had been easier to just ignore Jack's bravado. Now the threats were directed right at him. No doubt in Cole's mind he had grown bigger and stronger than Jack. Still, he had to worry about Jack's fighting experience. Slowly a resolve set in. It's time somebody stood up to the jerk. *Might get my butt kicked but I've had about enough.*

On Friday, the day of the track meet, Cole felt confident. For the first time in any competition he held nothing back. He won all four of his events and led his team to the county championship.

At the awards ceremony, after being given the trophy by a county commissioner, Mr. Hormel handed it to Cole and hoisted him onto his shoulders. The Brockton students and teammates chanted Cole's name over and over. Cole felt his face redden. His chest felt as if a dump truck were parked on it.

Filled with a mixture of pride and embarrassment, Cole struggled to breathe. From atop Mr. Hormel's shoulders, he looked up into the stands. A lone uniformed police officer sat in the top row of the bleachers. Cole saw the officer nod his head. He nodded back.

After the track meet, Cole rode his bike from the stadium across town to the projects. He cringed as he approached. Entering the governmental housing projects always affected him the same way. He was simply embarrassed to live there. Nothing he could do about it but it festered in his heart. His mom had told him the complex had originally been housing provided to the families of soldiers during World War II. It had since been converted by the town into low rent units for the poor. The isolated community at the edge of town consisted of a series of single story concrete block buildings each containing five separate living quarters. On countless bike trips Cole had counted forty separate buildings along short narrow streets named after World War II generals. In the center of the complex a community playground next to the administration building provided a recreation area for the kids.

As Cole entered the complex, he saw Jack and Dale Shaw and some other boys blocking the wide sidewalk leading in. Fences on either side meant Cole had to ride through them to get to his home. When he slowed to weave through the group, Jack bulled out of the crowd and grabbed the bicycle handle bars, stopping Cole. "I told you, sucker." Jack drew his fist back to throw a punch.

Cole leapt from his bike and pushed it into Jack, causing him to momentarily lose balance. Dale and several others jumped Cole knocking him to the ground. Jack regained his balance, threw the bike aside, and waded in. Others piled on top of Cole making it impossible to escape. The jumbled bodies also made it difficult for any blows to connect solidly. Cole knew sooner or later they would thin out and he would get his butt kicked for sure.

Struggling to do as much damage as he could, Cole punched with his one free hand. He heard several grunts of pain. Slowly he noticed his load becoming lighter. As he fought against those remaining, his eyes caught sight of Dave Thompson, a black kid on his basketball and track team, pulling boys off him. Dave didn't live here and Cole didn't know why he'd come--but was glad to see him.

Dave fended off several of the would-be fighters leaving only Jack and Dale for Cole to deal with. Still on his back with the two brothers on top of him, Cole managed to bring a free foot into Dale's stomach and he kicked out with all his might. Dale went sprawling backwards leaving only Jack still on top. Jack struck a hard blow to Cole's temple. Pain and panic surged through Cole's head. He twisted with all his strength and managed to break free and scramble to his feet. Once upright, Cole squared off with Jack. The others, now under Dave's daring eyes, watched and shouted. Dale's head was pinched in a headlock by one of Dave's long arms.

Cole had put up with Jack's crap long enough. He set his feet and tightened his jaw.

Jack bore in swinging. A fist caught Cole on the side of his face. The boys pummeled each other with mostly ineffective blows. Then Jack caught Cole with a straight left that brought blood trickling from his nose. Cole bobbed his head to avoid another straight punch. As they circled Cole started reading Jack's actions and judging his moves. After Cole blocked several punches, Jack yelled and charged in. He threw a roundhouse right at Cole's head. Cole ducked and came up with a vicious right of his own to Jack's stomach, doubling him over gasping for air. While Jack struggled for breath, Cole hooked a leg around one of Jack's and pushed him to the ground. Kneeling over him, Cole drew back his fist prepared to finish the fight. Jack threw up both hands to protect his face and said, "I give."

Cole, tense with anger and a bloody nose, wanted to hit him anyway, but slowly lowered his fist and got up. Can't violate the universal 'I give' rule. He walked to meet Dave as he released Dale and the others broke up. Cole noticed the disappointment on several faces as they ambled away. Wiping his bloody nose on his shirt sleeve, Cole called out. "Thanks, Dave. I thought..."

"Look out!" Dave shouted.

Jack rushed into Cole's back, knocking him to the ground again. Cole rolled as Jack tried to get him into a choke hold, and wrapped his long legs around Jack's mid-section. Cole squeezed with all his strength. Jack hung practically suspended over Cole, his eyes bulging as he fought to breathe.

After what seemed an eternity, Jack's face started turning blue and Cole released him. Jack lay on the ground moaning and panting. Cole rolled and jumped to his feet ready for another attack. But Jack got up slowly, turned, and slunk away, shoulders slumped and head down. When far enough away, Jack turned and called to Cole, "I'll get you for this, McKenna."

Cole turned back to his new ally. "I thought I was a goner for sure until you showed up, Dave. What were you doing here anyway?"

"My aunt lives in the projects. I came to visit her. It just didn't look like a fair fight, so I thought I'd help." Dave grinned.

"Well, I sure thank you," Cole said.

"What was that all about anyway, Cole?"

"Oh they were pissed because of the track meet. I always let them win races before and Jack thought he should have been in the track meet instead of me... and you, I guess. Jack told me earlier that if I didn't drop out, he'd beat me up. I guess he figured he'd need some help from the others."

"You think they'll lay for you again?"

"Yeah, maybe, but the others know I'd get them alone sometime and they won't have the nerve to do it without Jack."

Dave tapped Cole's shoulder. "I don't think Jack will try it alone now either."

Cole grinned, then sobered as he thought. "Boy I hope his older brothers don't come home for a while."

"Yeah, that could be big trouble. I've heard they're bad dudes," Dave said. "But I'd still try to stay away from Jack if I were you."

"You're probably right," Cole replied, then after an awkward pause, "If your aunt lives here, how's come I've never run into you here before?"

"When I was younger I was a little leery to come here by myself. Not too many black faces around here," Dave grinned. "I grew a little over last summer so now I'm not so afraid."

Cole looked up at the lanky kid. "I guess not."

After a short silence, Cole said, "You sure gave us a nice lead on that first leg of the relay."

Dave grinned. "Yeah, but by the time it got to you they were all about even again. George lost the third leg bad."

"I got lucky. I think Pleasant Valley ran their slowest guy as anchor."

"No way," Dave said. "They always put the fastest runner on anchor. That's why I was a little surprised when Mr. Hormel put you there after I blew by you at the qualification run. Did you pull up on purpose?" Dave raised his chin and eyebrows.

"I think I got a Charlie horse," Cole said, looking at the ground.

"Sure you did," Dave grinned. "Oh well, it worked out pretty good, huh?"

Cole smiled. "Yeah, I guess it did. You could have run the anchor leg better though. I think Mr. Hormel wanted us to have a lead."

The two boys shuffled around slightly ill at ease, not wanting to separate right away but not totally comfortable either. Cole felt drawn to his new friend and didn't know why. Sure he had helped him in the fight but it was more than that. They had played on the school basketball team and had always been friendly, but never close. Dave was a good sport and seemed shy like Cole. He didn't taunt others like some players. He often passed off when he could have shot. And he didn't brag or go through fancy antics when he scored. *Why haven't we been friends all along*? I guess it takes a fight to see what someone's made of.

"What are you doing this summer?" Cole finally asked.

"Not much, I guess. Go fishing mostly."

"Oh man, that's about all I do in the summer. How's come I've never run into you at the river?"

"Well it's a pretty big river," Dave said. "Where do you usually go?"

"I have several secret places," Cole grinned. "But mostly below the low dam north of town. How about you?"

"I usually go to a spot south of town close to my uncle's place."

"We'll have to go together sometime," Cole said.

"Yeah, that'd be great."

After another pause, Dave looked around and said, "Well I'd better get to Aunt Becky's. She'll be worried."

"Okay Dave. See you at school. And thanks again for helping out."

Dave turned back. "No problem, it was fun."

Monday morning Cole sat on the front steps at school waiting for Dave to show up. When he approached the building Cole saw the same wide smile as when they'd last parted. Cole stood and offered a high five. Dave smacked his hand as he went by then offered a low-five behind him which Cole matched. Together they entered the building. Their exchange sealed a bond between the two new friends.

Three

The summer Cole turned fifteen he got a job as stock boy at Bolton's Market. In the evenings after closing, he stayed late and cleaned the store. Every penny he earned he put aside for the dream car he planned to buy after his sixteenth birthday.

One of his substitute teachers, Mrs. Lutz, owned a farm and Cole had baled hay for them each summer, since sixth grade. Last year while roaming through the large barn, Cole discovered an old car under a tarp behind some other old equipment. When he uncovered it, he found a black 65 Mustang. He couldn't believe his eyes. He immediately started bugging Mr. Lutz about selling the car.

"You'd have to bale hay for the rest of your life to earn that car," Mr. Lutz laughed. Mr. Lutz explained that the car had belonged to their son, Jimmy, who died in Vietnam. After much good natured haggling for the past two years, and some help from Mrs. Lutz, he finally agreed to consider selling the car to Cole when he was ready. Each day and each dollar brought Cole another step closer to freedom.

Today when Cole arrived at work he noticed two police cruisers in the store parking lot. As he entered, Cole saw Mr. Bolton near the register talking to the officers. He turned down an aisle and started toward the back storage room. His mind filled with questions; he stopped when he heard Mr. Bolton call to him.

"Cole, come here a minute."

Cole shuffled back to Mr. Bolton and the officers. "Yes, Mr. Bolton?"

"The store was broken into last night. Somebody pried open the back. Did you see anybody hanging around the store when you left?"

Cole's head jerked up, eyes opened wide. "No, Sir. What'd they do?"

"Stole some cigarettes, candy, and beer, but mostly they trashed the place."

Cole looked around noticing shelf items in the aisles for the first time.

"What'd you do after you left work yesterday evening, Cole?" one of the officers asked.

"I, uhh..." A lump stated to form in his throat and his stomach tightened. "I uh, went home." Cole looked to Mr. Bolton, pleading. "We had to go to my Grandma's for supper." Oh God, Cole thought, they think I did it. His heart pounded in his chest.

"And when you returned?" the officer continued.

"Well, it was late--after nine, I think, cause we watched the last half of Cheers, then went to bed. Why?" Eyes wide he looked back and forth from the officer to Mr. Bolton

"Can anyone verify that story?" the other officer asked as he appeared from between the aisles.

Cole felt panic setting in when he looked up at the other cop. It was Officer Bradley, the same policeman who had come to his house when he was twelve. The same one who had nodded to him at the track meet. The same one who eyed him and waved from his cruiser, whenever their paths crossed--Cole's constant reminder of his criminal record.

"Uhh..." Cole struggled for composure, "I guess Mom could. And I sleep with my brother, so he could too." He turned to Mr. Bolton, his heart pounding and a lump in his throat. "I wouldn't do anything like this, Mr. Bolton."

"I know, Cole," Mr. Bolton said. "The officers are just checking out all possible details. Now you go on to the back room and start cleaning up the mess. We'll talk some more later."

Cole turned toward the rear of the store, controlling an urge to run.

"Wait a minute," the officer called out. "I don't want you to touch anything in the storeroom until we process the scene for fingerprints."

Cole stopped in his tracks. Fingerprints! His would be everywhere. They'd blame him.

Mr. Bolton said, "But Cole's prints will be on everything back there. He helps unload trucks and stocks the shelves. Hell mine will be too."

"We know that, Mr. Bolton," Officer Bradley explained, drawing his words out. "Look, we'll have to eliminate all prints that are yours and Coles... Anybody else handle items from the storeroom?"

Mr. Bolton put his hand to his chin. "Sometimes my wife, Millie, helps out."

"We'll need to get her prints as well." Officer Bradley turned to Cole. "Cole would you come with me for a minute while my partner talks with Mr. Bolton?"

"Sure," Cole said, following Bradley toward the soft drink machine. As they walked, Cole heard Mr. Bolton say to the other officer, "Cole's a good boy. Trust me he had nothing to do with this."

He breathed a sigh of relief. At least Mr. Bolton trusted him.

The officer fed coins into the slot, pulled out a root beer, and handed it to Cole. He repeated the process and popped the tab on his own soda. After a sip, he said, "Do you remember me, Cole?"

"Yes, Sir," Cole said, looking at the floor.

"Okay. My name is Bradley, Tom Bradley." He held out his massive hand and waited until Cole reluctantly shook it, then continued, "I doubt that you know, but I've been keeping track of you ever since that incident when you were twelve."

The panic showed in Cole's eyes, and the officer smiled. "Relax, Cole. I've been very impressed by the progress you've made since that little incident. You remember when I attended the elementary track meet where you destroyed the other kids? I felt a lot of pride for you that day." He grinned. "That onion thing really wasn't much of a crime, but those Shaw boys have caused us more trouble than they're worth but we couldn't arrest them without including you, and I think it might have done you some good, too," he dropped his chin and looked into Cole's eyes.

Cole refocused his gaze to the floor, not knowing what to say.

After a pause, Bradley said, "Cole did you know Mr. Hormel reported the garden incident and identified you boys that night?"

Mouth agape and eyes wide open, Cole's head jerked up.

"Yep," Bradley said. "He lives next door to the Turners. He told me later he was surprised to see you with the Shaws. He also told me he thought you were a good person and ordinarily you wouldn't be involved in anything like that."

Cole stood silent trying to digest what the officer said. Mr. Hormel hadn't given any sign that he knew of Cole's criminal past.

Bradley continued, "Look, I don't think you had anything to do with this break in, but we will have to eliminate you scientifically, so... Will you help us?"

Cole looked up. "How?"

"Well," Bradley explained. "We'll need your fingerprints for starters."

"Fingerprints?" Cole interrupted, almost pleading, "But...I've touched just about everything in the store."

"I know that. But again, we'll need your prints so we can tell which ones are yours and Mr. Bolton's, and then if we find any that don't match either of yours, we might have a suspect. So what do you think? Will you help?"

Cole's panic slowly gave way to a beginning excitement as he understood the officer's reasoning. "Sure I will," he said, holding out his hands, palms up.

"Not now," Bradley said, laughing. "We're not allowed to fingerprint juveniles without their parents' consent. Do you think your mother will allow us?"

"Oh, sure she will," Cole started, then thinking about his mother, added, "I think."

"Can we go to your house when we finish here and see what she says?"

"Well, Mom's not home. She works until three o'clock, and gets home about three thirty."

"Okay then, I'll come by your place about four o'clock. You tell her I'll be coming, and explain why. Maybe together we can solve this crime. Okay?"

"Okay," Cole said, feeling an unfamiliar excitement build.

Cole sipped his root beer as he watched two other men dressed in blue coveralls taking pictures, spreading black powder with little brushes, and pressing some sort of plastic stuff into the pry marks on the back door. He idly wondered how Officer Bradley knew root beer was his favorite soda pop. He quickly filed that thought as another demonstration of the same brilliance he'd noticed three years ago.

Four

Officer Bradley spent the next hour knocking on doors in the vicinity of Bolton's grocery. He routinely wrote down names of people who neither saw nor heard anything out of the ordinary--typical crime scene canvas. At one of the project units, Bradley recognized Mrs. Shaw. After she claimed to know nothing about the burglary, he asked, "Are any of your boys home, Mrs. Shaw?"

"Why?" she asked, squinting her eyes.

"Because, I'm asking all the kids around here. They play outside in the evenings and often see and hear things the adults don't. They might have some information that could help me on this."

"Dale and Larry are home. I guess I can get them." She turned and walked away. A few minutes later she returned with the boys. As soon as Dale saw the police officer, he twisted around as if to go back, but his mother clutched his arm and swung him back around to face the officer.

"Eugene and Jack are working and Glen's in summer school." She explained. "And the young ones weren't outside at all last night."

"That's all right," Bradley said, and then turned to Dale. "Hi, Dale. I'm Officer Bradley and I'm investigating a break-in at Bolton's market. Did you see or hear anything last night in the vicinity of the store?" Dale fidgeted and looked everywhere but at Bradley.

"Any noises or screeching tires near Bolton's?" he prodded.

"No," Dale said, with a scowl.

"Do you know anything at all about the break-in?"

"Now wait a minute," Mrs. Shaw protested. "My boys don't know nothin'. He already told you."

"Well, Ma'am, I'm just trying to get some help here. Maybe they heard something and didn't know what it was, or maybe they heard some talk about it. That's all I'm trying to find out."

Turning back to Dale, he asked, "How about it, do you know anything that might help me?"

"Well," Dale hesitated. He absently brought his right hand to his nose as his eyes shifted to the right. "Yeah, me and Jack heard McKenna say something about Bolton's. Yeah, he said he was gonna rip off old man Bolton some day,"

Now there's a lie if I ever saw one, Bradley thought. That body language is stronger than his words. "When did he say that, Dale?"

"Uh..." Dale stammered. "The other day, I guess."

"But the McKenna boy works for Mr. Bolton. Why would he want to do that?"

"Cause Bolton's a grumpy old ass and treats people like shit."

"And you and Jack both heard McKenna say that?"

"Yeah."

"Okay," Bradley said. "Mrs. Shaw when Jack gets home, tell him I'll need a statement from him as well. When do you expect him?"

"Whenever he gets here, I guess. You know how it is with teens."

"Well, tell him I'll drop by tomorrow to talk to him, all right?"

"Sure, I'll tell him."

Bradley returned to his cruiser and headed for the station to write up the report and wait for Mrs. McKenna to get home. This new twist had Bradley's suspicions aroused. Could he be wrong about Cole? He dismissed that thought when he considered the source of the information. Dale's body language had lie written all over it. Why did Dale lie? I just have to keep an open mind until I find the truth, he reminded himself.

~ * ~

When Cole's mother walked through the kitchen door, he rushed to her babbling, trying to get the entire story out in one sentence. She held up her hands to stop him as she put her purse on the table. "Whoa, slow down. What are you talking about?"

Cole started over. He told her about the break in at Bolton's and explained about the fingerprints. "Officer Bradley will be coming by later to get my prints. He needs your permission."

"What?" his mother's voice rose, "No way. He's not going to railroad you into this one. No way!"

"Wait, Mom. He knows I didn't have anything to do with the robbery, but he has to know which prints at the store are mine. He explained it all to me."

"I don't trust cops. And you shouldn't either. Remember the last time? You've got a record now you know."

"But Mom," Cole's shoulders slumped as he exhaled. "I was guilty of that one. I didn't have anything to do with this. Officer Bradley said he knows I didn't."

"So he says. I still don't like it."

"It'll be okay, you'll see."

When Officer Bradley arrived, he spent an extra fifteen minutes convincing Mrs. McKenna why he needed Cole's prints, after substantiating his whereabouts the night of the burglary. Finally, she acquiesced to his pleas.

With his portable ink pad, Bradley took prints of Cole's fingers and palms. When he finished he said, "By the way Mrs. McKenna, would you mind if I take a look around Cole's room so I can further eliminate him as a suspect."

Mrs. McKenna cocked her head and squinted. "What for?" she demanded.

"Well," Bradley began patiently, "So I can indicate in my report that with Cole's and your assistance, I checked his room and found nothing to connect him to this burglary. We have to eliminate him as a suspect."

"You mean he is a suspect?" Hands on her hips, she glared at the officer.

"No, Ma'am. It's complicated, but it'll help if we can totally rule him out. We'll be doing something similar at Mr. Bolton's house, and we sure know he didn't do this. Look," he added, "I'm sure Cole had nothing to do with this crime. He was with you the whole night, but we have to prove it, just like we have to prove in court that someone else did it."

Leading the officer to his bedroom, Cole said, "Sorry it's such a mess."

Bradley stopped at the doorway and looked around. It was indeed a mess. The bed hadn't been made; clothing littered the floor and bed. The pull down shade hung torn and loose at the top. The lone window had no curtains. The small room contained only a double bed and a chest-of-drawers, in addition to several plastic models and assorted toys and sports equipment strewn around.

Bradley walked to the chest and opened each drawer. He then looked in the closet moving things about to examine the contents. As he knelt to look under the bed, he froze in place. The officer looked up at Cole while withdrawing his handkerchief from his rear pocket. Bending back under the bed, Bradley withdrew two cartons of cigarettes, one at a time. He held them up so Cole and his mother could see.

Cole's mouth dropped open as his mother shrieked, "Oh, Cole, No! How could you?"

Cole stood stunned. His mind couldn't process what his eyes saw. The look on Bradley's face was hard and disappointed. Finally, Cole managed weakly, "I didn't do that." Pointing at the cartons, he added, "Those aren't mine."

Standing up slowly, Bradley studied Cole's eyes. They had a forlorn, pleading look but didn't waver from his. "Okay Cole," he put a large hand on Cole's shoulder. "Where's your brother?"

"No!" Cole said. "He didn't do it!"

"Now you're going to blame Mikey? My God, he's only nine years old." Mrs. McKenna put her hands to her head and started to cry.

"No, no. I'm not blaming Mikey." Bradley took off his hat and ran his hand through his hair. "Look, I just want to have additional verification that Cole was here all night. Bradley dropped his head for a moment. "I need to figure this all out."

Bradley took a long slow breath as he thought. He couldn't tell them about the Shaw boy's statement, and he hadn't talked to Jack yet, but something strange was going on here. Why would an intelligent boy like Cole steal from his employer, trash the place he knows he'll have to clean up, and then bring the evidence home and put it someplace where it would more than likely be found? Then give me permission to search--doesn't make much sense. According to Mr. Bolton's inventory, at least twenty cartons of cigarettes had been stolen. Where were the other cartons? And the beer? Something fishy here. Of course, Cole could have gotten up in the middle of the night without anyone knowing.

"Okay." Bradley finally said. "Let's all calm down here. I'm not jumping to any conclusions until the lab processes this evidence, and neither of you should either. Mrs. McKenna, Is anybody home here during the day? Where is Mr. McKenna?"

"God only knows. We separated a while back and I haven't seen him for some time. Last I heard he went to Atlanta to work with his brother painting houses, but knowing him and his brother, that won't last long."

"Anybody else who could have been here while you're at work?"

"Well just about the entire population of the projects. Have you seen the locks on these places? Mostly people don't even lock up anymore. You can get in with a credit card or a knife. Most of us don't have anything worth stealing anyway, so why bother. I leave the house before the boys get up so I doubt that they ever lock the door."

"Did you lock up when you left for work, Cole?" Bradley asked,

"No." Cole hung his head. "Aunt Helen came for Mikey, and I went to work."

"How about yesterday when you went to your grandma's? Did you lock the doors?"

Cole looked at his mother. She paused. "I didn't," she finally said.

Bradley thought some more before saying, "Okay. Again, don't be too upset over this. Until I have these cigarettes processed, I won't know anything." He looked into Cole's eyes. "I promise you I'll get to the bottom of it. I'll be in touch just as soon as I know something."

Five

The next day Cole pushed a cart with one wobbly wheel from the stockroom as Officer Bradley entered the store and approached Mr. Bolton.

When their eyes met, Bradley called, "Come up here a minute, Cole. I've got some news."

As Cole arrived at the register, he heard Bradley ask, "Mr. Bolton, does Cole stock all the cigarettes on the shelves?"

"Not all the time. He takes most of the deliveries and stacks the boxes in the storage room. But..."

Bradley furrowed his brow. "Doesn't he stock the shelves?"

"Oh, sure. But if he's busy, I sometimes get a few things for the shelves or display."

"That include cigarette cartons?"

"Sure, why?"

"Well," Bradley brought his hand to his chin, "that helps explain why Cole's prints were only on one of the cartons I took from his room."

Cole tensed.

"But on the other one," Bradley continued, "we found your prints but not Cole's." He glanced at Cole. "There were other prints on both cartons but we couldn't match them from our data base.

Cole stood stunned. All he heard was that his prints were on the stolen cigarettes. ...” He thinks I did it. Panic began setting in. “But...”

Mr. Bolton cut him off. “I told you Cole's prints would be everywhere in this store.”

“Yes, I know,” Bradley's voice had a touch of irritation, “but Cole's prints were only on one of the cartons I found in his bedroom.” He paused to let that register. “That means he couldn't have put them there. He would have had to touch both cartons.”

Cole sucked in a breath of relief.

“And,” Bradley continued, “if he had tried to wipe his prints off, he would have wiped the others off as well.” He turned to Cole and offered a smile.

Realization of what Bradley said slowly sank in. Cole's wide eyed, mouth agape look changed to a mouth open smile. He knew Officer Bradley could figure it out. He wanted to hug him, but forced himself to remain calm. “So who did it?” Cole asked. ”And how did they get in my room?”

Bradley shrugged. Well, son, that part we don't know yet, but I think I can make a pretty good case that it wasn't you. The other prints on the cartons aren't in our files. We're still waiting to hear from the FBI, but it'll be weeks before we hear back, and I don't think they'll have a match either.”

Cole shook his head, “FBI?”

Bradley smiled. “They keep a fingerprint data base for the entire nation. Much larger than ours.”

Bradley turned for the door. “Look,” he stated, “I still have some more investigating to do on this. Somebody in this neighborhood should have seen or heard something the night of the burglary.” He shook his head. “I'll stay in touch if anything turns up,” Bradley said, as he ambled toward the front door.

~ * ~

Bradley left the store and drove directly to the Shaw's unit. He couldn't share his thoughts with Cole and Bolton until he had some proof. But he had a strong suspicion who committed the burglary, as well as the frame job on Cole. He'd have to play this out to see if he could trip Jack up and obtain his prints.

Mrs. Shaw answered Bradley's knock with a sour look on her face.

"Good morning, Mrs. Shaw. I've come to talk to Jack. Is he home?" A scent of stale grease had greeted Bradley when she opened the door. It became worse when he stepped in.

"Yeah, but he's still in bed."

"Could you get him up please? I need his statement if I'm going to put the McKenna boy away."

She turned and went into the living room. She didn't return for several minutes and when she did, Jack and two younger brothers trailed behind, rubbing their eyes and blinking. Jack wore a pair of dirty jeans and no shirt or shoes. Both young brothers were in their underwear and sporting bad bed-hair.

"So Jack, Dale tells me you heard Cole McKenna say something about Bolton's. Tell me what you heard?"

"Yeah," Jack began with a sneer. His eyes pinched. "He said he was going to rip off old man Bolton."

"And when exactly did he say that?"

"A couple of days ago, I guess."

"Where were you guys when he told you?"

"Ah... well, I guess we was in the playground... yeah, by the swings."

"And what time of day was it, Jack?"

"Hell, I don't know. Why all the questions?"

"Look Jack, if I'm going to charge someone with a crime, I have to nail down all the little details. Was it daylight or night when he told you?"

"I don't remember." After a pause, Jack said, "Oh, yeah, it was almost dark. It was after the store closed, and it was the day before yesterday. Now you satisfied?"

"Okay, now we're getting somewhere. So that would have been the same evening that the store was burglarized, only the crime was done later that night. Is that right?"

"Yeah, that's when it was all right."

"Okay Jack, thanks for your help. I'll need you and Dale to testify at the trial after I make an arrest."

"No, I won't!" Jack's voice rose. "You can't make me. Hell, why don't you just go check McKenna's house? I'll bet the dumb ass has all the stuff right there."

"Jack, watch your mouth." Mrs. Shaw chastised.

"Oh, Ma. Shit."

"What makes you think that, Jack?" Bradley said, bringing him back on track.

"Well, he would, wouldn't he? I mean what else would he do with it? He's not too smart you know."

Bradley played him along a little more. "Yeah, I guess he would. I found his fingerprints all over the store."

"See, I told you he did it," Jack said with glee.

Bradley noticed Dale walk into the kitchen and lean against a wall with a grin plastered on his face.

"Speaking of prints, Jack, I'm taking prints of others who have frequented Bolton's just so I can eliminate them as possible suspects and hone in on McKenna. So would you mind if I took a sample of yours and maybe Dale's?" He nodded to Dale.

Being seventeen now and plenty street wise, Jack said, "No way man, I know my rights." He turned to his mother. "He can't make me do that. Ma, I know my rights. He can't make me."

"You got a warrant?" Mrs. Shaw asked with her chin raised.

"No, of course not," Bradley answered. "I've already got my suspect thanks to your boys here. I'm just trying to eliminate the others, that's all."

"Yeah, go get McKenna." Jack interjected. "He's the one you want. Why the hell you hassling us?"

"I'm not hassling you Jack; I'm just seeking your cooperation to bring a guilty party to justice. So, Mrs. Shaw, since the boys are juveniles, may I please have your permission to fingerprint Jack and Dale?"

"No way!" Jack protested, as Dale bolted toward the living room.

"No way," Mrs. Shaw echoed. "I know how you guys work, railroading innocent people and all. Now you go do your job, and leave my boys out of this."

Oh, they're in it all right, Bradley thought. Clear up to their ears. He left and drove back to Bolton's.

~ * ~

When he arrived at the store, Bradley explained the Shaw boys' statements to Mr. Bolton. "They've flat out accused Cole of the burglary, but I don't believe a word of it, especially now that we have the fingerprint evidence, and we can prove that Cole wasn't even home when they claim to have talked to him."

"Well, Officer, I know Cole, and I can assure you he would never do anything like this. Let me tell you a story. When Cole was ten, he found a lady's change purse along the path in that weedy field between here and the projects. Not a soul around to see him look in the purse. It contained the lady's grocery and rent money, well over a hundred dollars. Now almost any ten-year-old projects kid would have kept that money, but not Cole. He brought it here to me. Although there was no identification in the little change purse, I eventually found the lady and returned it. Now that's the kind of boy Cole is."

"Yeah, I've figured that out by now. I just wanted you to know what they said. And, I need to ask Cole a couple of questions. Is he here?"

"Sure." Bolton yelled toward the back. "Hey Cole, will you come out here, please?

Cole trotted up one of the isles to the register area. When he saw Bradley, a wide grin stretched his lips.

"Cole," Bradley began, "on the evening of the burglary, did you talk to the Shaw boys in the playground area?"

Cole thought. "No, Sir. Remember, I went straight to my grandma's right after work. Mom was ready to leave as soon as I walked in the door. Heck, I haven't seen Jack or Dale much at all this summer."

"Okay, Cole."

Turning to Mr. Bolton, he said, "For reasons I can't divulge, it's beginning to look like the Shaw boys might be my prime suspects here, but I'll never prove it unless I can find a witness or somehow get their fingerprints."

"Can't you just go get them?" Cole asked, "You know like you did mine."

"No Cole. Remember, I had to have you and your mother's permission to take your prints, and Mrs. Shaw wouldn't give her consent. You see Cole, police officers have certain rules that we must follow in order to get evidence admitted into court, and that's one of them concerning juveniles." Bradley paused thinking how much he should try to explain. "Now if I could find an object that someone touched and left around in a public place, then I would be free to take prints from it, but that's not likely to happen. So I'm stuck I guess."

Bradley thought a moment then said, "Mr. Bolton, do the Shaw boys ever come in here and drink a soda and leave the bottle or can here?"

"No," Bolton said. "I don't allow them or anyone to drink in the store. I don't want to encourage that sort of hanging around."

"Well it was worth a shot." Bradley said. "Although, it would be a way to get their prints and bypass the rules a little." Bradley turned to the front door and waved over his head. "I'll keep you informed if I learn anything."

~ * ~

Cole's mind churned. Maybe he could figure out a way to help.

After Officer Bradley left the store, Cole approached his boss. "Mr. Bolton, could you get along without me for a while? I've got something to do."

Mr. Bolton looked at him quizzically for a second. "Now Cole, you know you can't confront the Shaw boys, don't you? Officer Bradley told us things in confidence and if you go and tip his hand he might never get the evidence he needs."

"Oh, no, I wasn't going to do anything like that, but I've got an idea that just might help him out."Bolton eyed Cole again, "I don't think you should get involved in this."

"I already am involved in it, Mr. Bolton. I have to try something. I promise I'll be careful."

"Well, I stocked these shelves by myself before you came, so I guess I can do it again. Besides, the big deliveries don't come until Monday. How long do you need, Cole?

"I don't know, but a couple of days should do it."

"Mr. Bolton looked into Cole's eyes. "What do you have planned, young man?"

"I don't know exactly, but I've got to try something."

"Okay, Cole." He placed both hands on the boy's shoulders. "But you be careful, and don't interfere with Officer Bradley's investigation."

"Oh, I won't."

Six

That afternoon found Cole headed for the rear of the Community Center which offered a clear view of the Shaw's unit. Set next to the basketball court at the rear of the office building, the recreational area had followed the neighborhood's slow decline. A low sagging fence surrounded the area. The rusted jungle gym sat near a tilting merry-go-round.

Four boys, around eight or nine, played cops and robbers between the rusted swing sets and the twisted jungle-gym in the dusty playground. Cole cut through the boy's mock gun battle and drew little attention as he headed for the large gnarly maple tree at the rear of the play area. Dust swirled as the boys ran and shouted "Bang!" A glance around, as Cole ran, confirmed the kids had paid no attention to him. A few strides later, he launched himself up to a tree branch about eight feet off the ground. He kipped up and grabbed the next handhold.

Another twelve feet up, he straddled the tree's main fork and settled in to watch the Shaws' back door. His view included the end of the building in case they used the front door. As the afternoon wore on, Cole wished he'd brought something to read. He fidgeted to ease his cramped butt. Just before dusk his patience was rewarded when Dale and Jack emerged with a loud bang of the door. Mrs. Shaw's scream of protest followed her sons, who laughed as they ran.

Cole slid down the tree as soon as he saw the brothers head for the main road. He followed at a distance, hiding behind trees, buildings, and cars as he shadowed the boys. They led Cole out of the complex and headed for the dilapidated warehouse district south of the projects. When Dale whirled around, Cole banged his shin on the bumper of an abandoned car as he skirted back to his cover. Both hands clasping his leg, Cole gritted his teeth against the pain. He risked a peek through the car windows. They had continued on, so Cole jumped up and limped to his next vantage point.

From behind a dumpster, Cole watched Jack and Dale stroll down an alley in the rear of an abandoned building. A musty smell like rotting carpet mixed with rancid garbage assaulted Cole's nostrils. He tried breathing through his mouth. It didn't help much. The brothers entered an open door. Cole waited, not knowing what to do next. If he went in the door and they were still there, they'd see him. While trying to figure out his next move, he heard hoots and laughter coming from a broken window on the second floor. Cole focused all his attention on the muted conversation. It sounded like Jack and Dale. He ran for the door.

Once inside, he paused to allow his eyesight to adjust to the low light. A concrete and metal staircase, leading up, stood a few paces in front of him. Delicately he ascended the stairs. When he neared the second floor, he could hear them talking more clearly. It was Jack and Dale for sure. Easing onto the landing, he saw a series of doorways along a hallway. Some doors stood open, and some rooms had no doors at all. Cole isolated the voices coming from a room two down to his right. He quickly snuck along the hall to the room where the voices were and peeked through the crack on the hinge side of the partially opened door. Cole stood in the dark hallway and peered into a room dimly lit by a south window. He saw Jack and Dale smoking and drinking beer from long neck bottles.

Cole's excitement raged. He had them now. He couldn't stay in the hallway though. Sooner or later they'd spot him or when they left he'd have to make a run for it. He needed that evidence. He decided to hide and wait. Cole eased into the next room along the hall. This room didn't have a window and was dark. Feeling his way along the adjacent wall connecting the two rooms, Cole tripped over something and stumbled. His heart froze in his chest. From the next room he heard Jack cry out, "What the hell was that?"

After a tense moment, Cole squatted and felt around the floor. He had tripped over a large cardboard box. He sat with his back to the wall and gently pulled the box in front of him. *Lot of good this will do.*

He heard Jack say, "Go see what made that noise, Dale."

Scarcely breathing, Cole heard footsteps echoing on the concrete. A door slammed. Heels clanging on the floor came nearer. The box is too small to hide me if he has a light. He tried to make his body smaller. The steps stopped, then faded the other direction. He heard Dale's voice call out, "Probably that damn old cat that hangs out around here. If I catch it, I'll kill it."

When Cole could hear nothing but the voices in the other room he breathed out the air he had held. He leaned against the wall and tried to relax. Through the adjacent wall he could hear laughter, but couldn't understand anything else.

Cole waited for what seemed an eternity, and then finally heard footsteps on the concrete floor. He listened as the voices faded down the hall. He waited until he was sure they had left the building then eased back to the room they'd been in and looked inside. This room was similar to the one in which he had hidden, except for the window that stood open. A stained, torn mattress lay on the floor against the wall on his left. A broken-down couch with no cushions sat crookedly along the wall to his right, and a battered metal desk stood near the window. Cigarette butts littered the floor. Another door opened off the back wall near the mattress. Cole walked toward that door. As he passed the desk he saw a large fifty-five gallon drum full of trash. On top of an old Pizza box in the trash drum he saw two beer bottles. That's it, he thought. No other bottles were visible in the room.

He continued to the other door and opened it. The room had no windows. Probably a storage room or large closet. The dim light from the main room didn't help. He couldn't see anything. He felt the wall for a light switch. Flipped it--nothing.

Not wanting to repeat his last stumble, walking in a dark room, Cole crawled on his hands and knees to explore. He slowly probed his way around the small room. Despite his efforts to be careful he bumped into something with his hand and heard what sounded like bottles toppling. He froze as his heart jumped into his throat. The noise echoed off the bare walls of the hollow room sounding as loud as a traffic crash to his ears. He remained still a moment then decided not to risk further noise. He knew the beer bottles in the trash were what he had come for, so he stood and backed out of the small room.

It was time to notify Officer Bradley, but he couldn't leave the evidence here, they might come back and clean it out.

Having seen enough cop shows on TV, Cole knew better than to just grab the beer bottles. He sure didn't want his fingerprints on them. He looked around the room for something in which to put the evidence, but found nothing. Finally, he stuck an index finger into each neck and lifted them out of the drum. Holding them upside down caused a trickle of beer to run down his fingers and hands. With the upside down bottles in front of him, Cole headed for home, keeping a watch out for the Shaw brothers, and hoping no one else would see him.

When Cole arrived at his kitchen door, he kicked the door with his foot until his brother opened it. He tilted the bottles right side up on the kitchen table and after admonishing Mikey not to touch them, called to his mother.

"Quick, Mom, call Officer Bradley and tell him I have the evidence he needs."

"What are you talking about?" then spotting the two beer bottles on the table said, "Oh Cole."

"What?" he said, brow furrowed. "Oh, they're not mine. That's the evidence for Officer Bradley.

"What?" she repeated.

"Just call Officer Bradley, will you Mom?"

"Cole," she explained, "Officer Bradley works the day shift and it's now after eight. I'm sure he's not working."

"Oh, yeah, I forgot," Cole said.

He looked around the kitchen and then went to the cabinet under the sink and retrieved a paper grocery bag. Sticking his index fingers back into the bottles he placed them in the large sack. Glaring at his mother and brother Cole ordered, "Don't anybody touch that sack until Officer Bradley can get here."

Seven

The next morning Cole woke as his mother readied for work. He had barely slept through the excitement burning inside him. "Mom, can you call Officer Bradley now?"

"No." She looked at him and frowned. "He won't be at work until probably seven or eight o'clock. You call then and tell them you need to see him." Before she left, she found the police department number in the directory and wrote it on a note pad.

Cole sat at his kitchen table staring at the wall clock. At seven o'clock sharp he dialed the number his mother left for him.

"Brockton police department, may I help you?"

"Hello," Cole said. I need to talk to Officer Bradley please."

"I'm sorry, Officer Bradley isn't here. His shift starts at eight o'clock. Do you need an officer? Is this an emergency?"

Yes, it's an emergency, Cole thought. "No, Ma'am. I just need to talk to Officer Bradley."

"What is your name and number? I'll leave him a message"

Cole gave her the information and gazed at the clock as he hung up. Almost another hour. What if Bradley didn't get the message? Cole twitched with excited impatience.

The hands of the clock passed the eight o'clock mark. Cole's hand rested on the phone receiver. At twenty after eight he lifted the receiver to dial the number again. A knock at the door made him jump and drop the phone.

He saw a large uniformed body in the door window. He leapt to the door and opened it for Officer Bradley. "What's up, Cole?"

"Come in and see what I've got," Cole said, bursting with enthusiasm.

Bradley grinned. "Must be something really important. Whatcha' got?"

"Well, you said you needed to get Jack and Dale's fingerprints, and I got them for you." His upturned face bore a wide satisfied smile.

"You what?" Bradley said.

"Yeah," Cole explained. "I followed them yesterday and found their hiding place. I got these two beer bottles with their prints on them." He quickly retrieved the paper sack and opened it.

Bradley stared, mouth agape at the bottles then back to Cole, then back to the bottles again. He didn't speak. His eyes squinted and his brow furrowed. "Slow down, Cole, and tell me exactly what happened."

Cole relayed the story of his surveillance and how he found the evidence. When he told the part about using his fingers in the bottle openings, Bradley chuckled. "What on earth made you do that, Cole?"

"I watch the cop shows on TV and they're always careful not to mess up the evidence."

After a long pause, Bradley said, "Cole, I told you yesterday about some of the rules we have to go by. They're important. This evidence will be questionable in court. If it had been me who followed them, and I had seen them touch the bottles, I could testify to that." Bradley tilted his head in thought. 'The bottles were left in a place where Jack and Dale had no reasonable expectation of privacy, so that part's good. But again, I can't testify to any of that."

Cole's enthusiasm crashed. "You mean I didn't do any good?"

"No I don't mean that at all." Bradley paused again. "Look, Cole, you shouldn't have done what you did." He lowered his head and held Cole's eyes. "You could have been hurt. But since you did it...well, it just might help. I just don't think we can use it in court. But that's not the end of it. Can you show me where you found these bottles?"

"Sure." Cole brightened.

"Understand, Cole, this still won't be the absolute proof we need, since I didn't see them there with the beer." He paused a moment, then continued while thinking out loud. "Now wait a minute, there might just be a way, but you'd have to testify in court that you followed the boys, saw them drink from these bottles, and then you collected the evidence." Bradley put his hand to his chin and stroked it. "Did you see them put the bottles in the trash can?'

"N... no. But they were the only ones in that room, and I did see them drinking from beer bottles. I think the ones in the closet were full."

After another pause, Bradley continued, "I don't know if it's been done before, but the chain of custody of evidence should apply to a citizen the same as it does to police officers. It might just work. I'll have to talk to the prosecutor to see what he thinks."

Cole's excitement began to build again.

Bradley picked up the grocery bag holding the bottles. "Okay, show me where you found these."

From the passenger seat of Bradley's cruiser, Cole gave directions to the alley alongside the abandoned warehouse. Bradley followed Cole into the rear door and up to the second floor using his flashlight to light the way. Together they examined the room. Bradley looked into the trash barrel and casually reminded Cole, "Don't touch anything."

When he flashed his light into the rear storage room he saw several unopened cartons of cigarettes and a number of long necked bottles of beer along one wall. Some of the bottles were tipped over. Back in the main room, Bradley keyed the mic on his portable radio to notify the dispatcher to send the evidence technicians to the location.

~ * ~

The case was a slam dunk. The lot numbers on the beer and cigarettes matched the inventory of the store. Both Jack's and Dale's prints were on the bottles and cigarette cartons, as well as on the rear door of the store. Dale Shaw's fingerprints were on both cartons of cigarettes found under Cole's bed. The evidence technicians recovered a paper grocery bag from the bottom of the warehouse trash can that matched the brand used by Bolton's. Cole's testimony that he had seen both brothers smoking and drinking at the warehouse was more than enough to establish probable cause for their arrest.

The court appointed attorney for the Shaws argued they had simply found the stolen items in the warehouse and their prints were put on the items after they found them. He further pointed out they had been in the store many times and their prints could have been put there at any time. The judge did not buy the arguments. Considering the brother's extensive juvenile records, the judge sentenced each to a six month term in juvenile detention.

As the bailiff led the brothers out of the courtroom, Jack turned and glared at Cole. "I'll get you for this McKenna!" he called out, before the bailiff could turn him toward the side door.

Officer Bradley put his arm around Cole's shoulders and guided him out of the court room. "Don't pay much attention to him, Cole. He's just blowing off steam."

"I know," Cole said. "He don't scare me anymore."

"Doesn't," Bradley admonished.

"Doesn't what?" Cole asked.

"Doesn't scare me--not don't."

"He doesn't scare you either?" Cole grinned up at Bradley, knowing what he'd meant but unable to resist.

Bradley playfully slapped him on the head, and both laughed.

Eight

The excitement of the trial waned rapidly for Cole. With Jack and Dale gone and school about to start, he had little time to revel in past events. He still worked at Bolton's market and would continue to do so in the evenings after school. This weekend he and Dave were baling hay for the Lutz's as they had every summer since seventh grade.

The tractor rounded the far end of the barn laden with the final load of hay bales stacked six high. Mr. Lutz stopped near the barn and shut the engine down. Cole and Dave sat on lower hay bales. Their sweat and dust soaked shirts hung limp with the weight of moisture, dust, and alfalfa pollen. Mrs. Lutz appeared from the kitchen door and headed out to greet them in the hot August sun. Rivulets of condensation running down the sides of the pitcher in her hand, mirrored the streams of perspiration dripping from Cole's and Dave's foreheads.

From their perch on the hay wagon they watched with salivating anticipation as Mrs. Lutz carefully trod the path to the barn. With the afternoon sun at her back, her well rounded small frame topped by a crown of cotton-candy white hair gave the appearance of an apparition approaching. Both boys launched themselves from the wagon, pulled off their already wet gloves and wiped their brows.

From her apron pocket, Mrs. Lutz produced three plastic glasses and handed them each one. The sound of ice and liquid pouring into the glasses sounded like a symphony to Cole's ears. He practically drained his glass in one gulp. He and Dave sat on the edge of the trailer tongue while Mr. Lutz stayed seated on the tractor. In time each held his glass out for a refill.

"You boys looking forward to your sophomore year of high school?" Mrs. Lutz asked, refilling Dave's glass.

"Yes, Ma'am," Dave said. Good thing we're getting this hay in now. Football practice starts next week."

"Oh, you boys going out for the team?"

"Yeah," Cole said. "We both played some last year. This year should be a good one now that we'll be varsity. He and Dave laughed as they elbowed each other, spilling some of Cole's iced tea.

"Well, we think we'll be varsity anyway," Dave finally said.

Mrs. Lutz clucked and shook her head as she looked over her glasses as if in mock disapproval of their horse play. She turned for the house and called over her shoulder, "Supper in about an hour. Don't forget to wash up."

Mr. Lutz drained his glass and placed it in the cup holder dangling from the instrument panel. He turned to the wagon. "You still saving up for that old Mustang, Cole?" he asked with a knowing grin. "You'll be sixteen soon, won'tcha?"

"Not for a few months yet, but I've got over a thousand dollars in my savings account."

"Wow. A thousand huh? How much you reckon you'll have by your birthday?"

"Well if you paid us more, I'd probably have enough."

Dave offered a high five and Cole smacked it.

Mr. Lutz shook his head and laughed with them. He jumped from the tractor and motioned for the boys to help him hook the conveyor belt to the drive pulley so they could transfer the baled hay to the barn loft.

"Mr. Lutz... how much do I need to buy the Mustang? You never said a price."

"You just keep saving your money, boy. When you're thirty you might have enough." Mr. Lutz laughed and slapped his leg.

"You boys go up in the mow and I'll feed the bales on the conveyer. You know the drill."

~ * ~

After supper, Cole and Dave went to the barn and removed the tarp from Cole's dream car, a ritual they did on every trip to the farm. Both stared at the jet black 65 Mustang as if it were a religious symbol. One on each side, they reverently ran their hands along the body lines until they got to the doors. They opened them simultaneously and eased into the bucket seats. Neither spoke. Cole's left hand rested on the steering wheel and his right gripped the miniature chrome piston someone had attached to the four-speed floor shift. He dreamed of the open highway. Dave's face registered a similar far off look.

After a spell of silence and exploration of the interior, a sound caught Cole's attention. He looked up. Mr. Lutz stood in the shadows of the far corner of the stall. His head down and shoulders slumped. Cole nudged Dave and nodded. They got out of the car and headed for Mr. Lutz.

"Sorry, Mr. Lutz. We just wanted to see it again," Cole said. As he neared, he noticed tears streaking down the man's face.

"It's okay, Cole. I was just thinking about Jimmy." His usual booming voice now subdued to almost a whisper.

Cole didn't want to cause Mr. Lutz any more pain but thought he might want to talk about his son. "What happened, Mr. Lutz? You never told us."

Mr. Lutz looked up but didn't speak. He blinked and gave a quick jerk of his head. "It's hard to talk about, Cole. You'll understand some day."

"I'm sorry. I didn't mean to pry."

"No, I guess you should know. That old car was as important to him as it is to you." He closed his eyes and dropped his head. Cole and Dave stood silent.

Mr. Lutz looked up with resolve on his face. "Boys, that Vietnam was a bad war. We probably shouldn't have been involved in it. In the beginning we thought we should fight against communism. And maybe we should have, but our country hadn't been attacked and there wasn't much support for our involvement or our troops. Hell, some people spit on our soldiers when they came home. For some reason our political leaders and even our military didn't fight that war to win. They just kept sending our boys over there to get killed. And that's what happened to Jimmy."

"Do you know how it happened?" Cole almost whispered.

"Yep, the Army sent a detailed report of the action when he was killed." Mr. Lutz paused and took a deep breath. "Don't know how true it is. Sometimes I think they just make up a story to ease the pain for us at home. They did award him a bronze star and a purple heart for heroic action and bravery during battle, though. So what they said must have some truth to it."

"Wow," Dave said. "What'd he do?"

"They said his squad was ambushed by a company of Viet Cong rebels in a jungle battle. They were pinned down with little cover. The radioman had been shot and lay in a clearing in full view of the enemy. Jimmy..." Mr. Lutz paused, mouth open and heaved a couple of breaths. "They said Jimmy left his cover and ran to the radioman. When he tried to use the radio, to call in air support, he was shot..." His voice trailed off. "But he managed to call in the choppers." He paused again for a breath. His voice cracked. "And when Jimmy tried to crawl back to cover he was shot again and killed." Cole saw Mr. Lutz's face hardened as he clamped his jaw. "Air support came in time and routed the Viet Cong. They said if it hadn't been for Jimmy the entire squad would have been slaughtered."

The three of them stood in silence.

From a distance, Mrs. Lutz's sing-song voice called, "Harold."

"Oops, I'd better see what she wants. Don't forget to cover that car back up boys."

Cole and Dave pulled the tarp back over the Mustang and walked outside.

"Well boys it's your lucky day. She says I have to drive you home. It's too near dark to be riding your bikes."

"No," Cole started to protest. "We can make it before dark."

"Not a chance, Cole. You'll learn someday, when the missus says to do something, it's better to just do it. Now pile them bikes in the back of the pick-up and let's get going."

Nine

Three weeks into their sophomore year, Cole and Dave walked the hall from English class headed for Social Studies. That morning in home room Dave had been elected class president. They talked of that and the upcoming football game tonight. Cole abruptly stopped and grabbed Dave's arm. "Look." He turned his head to the right. A girl leaned against the stair railing studying a paper while balancing a load of books cradled in her other arm. "Who's that?" he asked, still unable to take his eyes off the girl. Bright sunlight, streaming through a bank of windows behind the stairwell, framed her with a golden glow. Light caramel hair to her shoulders sparkled in the rays. Gauged by the height of the stair rail, she looked tall, maybe five-eight or nine, trim and athletic. Her jeans were snug and her V-neck sweater appeared to be strained from within.

Dave stared in awe as well. "Don't know. I've never seen her before."

Cole swallowed, took a deep breath, and silently eased away from Dave toward the girl, as if drawn by a magnetic force. As he walked, his eyes drank in every detail. He stood in front of her until she looked up from her paper. Shockingly light, almost violet, eyes stared back at him. Cole froze. He couldn't rip his gaze from those eyes.

When her brows furrowed, he finally found his voice. "You... ah, look stressed out. Can I help you?" he stammered.

Her head tilted up, she said, "I think I'm lost. I just changed English classes and I can't seem to find 208 B. This map is confusing."

Ah, Freshman English, Cole thought. That's why I haven't seen her before. "Hallway B is on the far side of the gym. It's the new addition. Just go to the end of this hall and turn right. At the other end, turn right again and 208 B is about half way down."

"Thank you." She shuffled the books in her arm and attempted to insert the map into one. Some papers fell from her load. Her face pinched and her shoulders slumped. They both started to bend at the same time. Cole's arm bumped the books in her arm and they clattered to the floor. She stood frozen, mouth agape. Cole dropped to the floor and gathered books and scattered papers in a rush. When he handed them to her, he knew his face must be red; he felt the heat. "Sorry," he mumbled.

She hurriedly tried to organize the mess. "It's okay, she said with a dejected tone. "Oh crap, I'm going to be late." She turned to go.

"Wait," Cole said. "What's your name?"

"Erin," she said, walking away at a rapid pace. After a couple of steps she looked back and waved. "Thanks."

Cole watched until she rounded the corner at the end of the hall.

"Well?" Dave's brows raised and both hands opened palms up as he approached Cole.

"Well, what?" Cole drew his eyes back to Dave.

"Who is she?"

Cole breathed out a sigh. "Erin." He drew it out. "She's a freshman, I think."

Dave waved his hand in front of Cole's face. "Yoo-hoo, McFly, anybody home? You look like you're on another planet."

Cole shook his head. "Wow, she's smoking hot."

"Yeah, yeah. Too hot for you, especially after that suave approach. Come on, we'd better get to class."

At lunch, between bites of his cardboard hamburger, Cole trailed his eyes over the cafeteria crowd trying to spot the mystery girl. The third time Cole stood to get a better look, Dave grabbed his arm and pulled him down to the bench. "You'd better get a grip man; we've got a game tonight. Can't have your head up your butt."

"I know." Cole gave a little jerk and pursed his lips. "I just want to know who she is."

"You know who she is. Erin--Freshman. Duh, remember?" Dave opened his eyes wide and let his mouth hang. "You just want to know if she's available and willing."

"Do not. Hell, I don't even know her last name.

"Hey buddy, as your president I'm going to have to issue an executive order. No thinking about girls until after football season." Dave had a pleased look of superiority on his face.

"President. You can't even spell it. The only reason they elected you was because I nominated you. That and the fact that you stood out as the only black guy in the room."

"Don't forget my wonderful speech."

"Speech? You mumbled something about coming up from slavery and ended with 'We shall overcome'. Nobody bought that crap."

"They wrote my name down."

"Yeah, well it was a sympathy vote."

Dave's face and voice took on a more serious tone. "Girls can be a distraction, Cole. Coach said so."

"I don't even know who she is. Relax. You're probably right; she wouldn't give me the time of day."

That night the Brockton Broncos won their third game in a row. Cole threw for over a hundred yards with one touchdown pass to

Dave, and rushed for another 83 yards. Two other touchdowns were scored by the fullback and the running back. Brockton was not scored on. So far the defense had allowed only two touchdowns.

When Cole stepped out of the communal shower with a towel wrapped around his waist he found Dave dressed and posing. He held the flaps of a cream colored sport jacket out to expose a tan polo shirt and brown slacks. His jheri curls glistened in the florescent lights. Cole bent and laughed. "What is that?"

Dave affected a perplexed look. "It's my new Miami Vice look. Whaddaya think?"

Cole just shook his head. "If you had a big hat, you'd look like a pimp."

"Aw man, that hurts."

As Cole dressed, Dave said, "And you're going to a dance dressed like that?

"What?" Cole looked down at his tan polo shirt, khakis, and brown Doc Marten's.

"You need a big pair of horn rimmed glasses to complete the nerd look."

Cole put his hand to his chest as if stabbed. "Just wait and see if I throw anything your way next week."

Cole and Dave left the locker-room jostling each other and headed back to the school for the Friday dance. The gym was full by the time they arrived. A student DJ wanna-be chattered into a microphone between songs. They saw a group of football players gathered at a table and headed their way. High-fives, laughter and good natured jibes flew.

After they'd settled, Jason Jinks, the senior quarterback Cole had beaten out for the starting position, grabbed him by the arm and led him aside. "Hey, Cole," he leaned in close and lowered his voice. "I've got some beer in my car. Want to join me for a little celebration?"

Cole jerked his head up, a puzzled look on his face. "No... thanks. I don't do that."

"It's just beer. What are you, a wuss?"

"Yeah, I guess so." Cole pulled his arm away and went back to the table.

"What was that all about? Dave asked.

"I'll tell you later." Cole perused the crowd. When his eyes fell on Erin sitting with a table of freshmen girls, he froze. He almost didn't recognize her. Her hair was crimped almost frizzy and held to one side by a large banana clip. Long earrings dangled almost to her shoulders.

After a moment, Cole rose and walked away from Dave without a word. He felt Dave's eyes follow his progress around the perimeter of the dance floor.

She must have seen him coming. A slight smile showed on her face and she stood before he got to the table. Cole ambled up glancing alternately from his feet to Erin. When he arrived he was struck numb. She looked stunning in a charcoal blouse tucked into a short ruffled white skirt over black leotards with white leggings. His lips wouldn't move and his brain refused to think. The other girls at the table watched the pair with anticipation. Erin broke the awkward silence. "Yes, I'd love to dance."

She looped her arm through his and led him to the dance floor. I'm an idiot, his brain chided. Thank God it's a slow song, Cole thought. At least Mom had shown him some of the basics of slow dancing.

They swayed together through the dance in silence. Cole's brain activity was so hectic his voice couldn't have worked anyway. Should I move my hand? It's kind of low. No, if I move it she'll think I'm trying to grope her. God this is different than dancing with Mom. Should I back off a little? My chest is against her boobs. Oh no. Think football, think football.

When the song ended, Cole expelled a breath and led her to the drink table. He picked up a plastic cup filled with soda and handed it to her.

"I have one at the table, but thank you." Her eyes twinkled in the lights. "You're not going to knock this out of my hand are you?"

Cole felt the heat build. "I ah, hope not."

Cole took a drink from his cup and a deep breath, trying to get some nerve. "Erin... I know you don't know me very well, and... well, we just met and everything."

She set her drink on the table and gazed at him in earnest.

"Anyway... I was wondering if you'd like to go to a movie with me sometime?" The words came out rapidly so he couldn't stop them.

She paused with a quizzical look on her face. "I don't know." She seemed to be studying him "This is kinda sudden, isn't it? I don't even know your name."

"Oh, damn. Oops, sorry. It's Cole, Cole McKenna."

She put her hand to her face and gave a little laugh. "Yeah, I know. The girls told me. You're the quarterback." Before Cole could answer, she stuck out her hand and said, "Hi, Cole. I'm pleased to meet you." Her hand felt like warm velvet against Cole's. A period of silence followed.

They simultaneously reached for their drinks. Cole looked down at her. "Well, I just didn't want to miss a chance. I understand if you don't want to. I just feel like I'd like to get to know you."

"What's to know? I'm just a freshman. I'm sure a big football star like you wouldn't be interested in anything I have to say." She looked coyly at him. "Or are you interested in something other than my brain?" Her look changed to accusatory.

Cole felt his face burning again. "No. I mean yes. I mean... you're confusing me." He put a hand to his forehead and squeezed. "I guess I made a mistake. If you don't want to go out with me..."

"Whoa," she held up her hand. "I didn't say that. I was just kinda messing with you." She had a playful smile on her lips. "I'm allowed to date this year, but I have rules."

What?" Cole almost spilled his drink. "You mean you'll go with me? What rules?"

I have to be in by ten o'clock and I'm not allowed to be in a car. My dad can be mean sometimes." She had a pout on her lips.

That doesn't sound too encouraging. What am I getting into here? "Ah, well, I don't drive yet and we could go to an early movie."

"I'll have to ask my parents, but if they say it's all right, I'd love to. When do you want to go?"

Cole hadn't thought that far ahead. "Ah, how about tomorrow?"

She smiled. "Okay, I'll ask Dad."

"Wow. That's great. How will I know if it's okay?"

Erin put her glass down and looked around. A clipboard with a pencil attached by a string lay on the end of the long table. She reached for it and one of the cocktail napkins. She quickly scrawled her phone number on a napkin. When she finished, she handed it to Cole. "Call me tomorrow, and don't lose this," she teased.

"Okay if I ride my bike to your house, then we can walk to the movie?"

"Sure. That will be perfect," she said.

Cole felt joy surging but apprehension tried to push it aside. What about her dad?

A noise drew their attention to the other end of the gym. Folding metal chairs clattered to the floor amid shouting. A swarm of teens swayed back and forth knocking more chairs over. It came from the table where the football players were.

"Excuse me," Cole said, turning for the skirmish.

When he got there, Coach Wion held Jason in a bear hug from behind and a group surrounded Dave, who sat on a chair with his hands to his face.

Ten

Cole pulled and pushed teammates aside until he got to Dave. "You okay, Bro? What happened?"

Dave looked up, his left eye starting to swell. "Yeah, I'm okay. He," nodding toward Jason, "sucker-punched me. Then these assholes grabbed me before I could get to him."

Cole glared at the teammates around Dave. His fists clenched and unclenched as his anger built.

"Whoa, Cole. We saw the coach coming," one of them offered.

Cole turned toward Jason but Coach Wion was dragging him away. Cole moved to follow, but Dave reached a long arm out and grabbed him. "Wait, Cole. Not worth it now."

Cole sucked in a big breath and looked back to the teammates near Dave. "Yeah," he said. Sorry guys. You probably did the right thing. No sense in Dave getting in trouble too."

The din around them grew as students rushed to see what had happened.

The sound system squealed when Mr. Ervin, the assistant principal, apparently put his mouth too close to the mic. But it got everyone's attention. The authoritative voice they all listened to during morning announcements said, "Attention all students. The dance is now over for tonight. Let's all head home."

A collective groan, followed by an assortment of cat calls bounced off the walls of the gym.

Mr. Ervin continued, "It's all over folks. I want the gym cleared in the next few minutes, unless you want to spend the next week sitting in the in-school suspension room."

The noise of student complaints and metal chairs screeching echoed through the auditorium.

As students shuffled toward the exits, Mr. Ervin appeared at Dave's table. "You okay, Dave?"

"Yeah, I guess so."

While Mr. Ervin talked to Dave, Cole scanned the exiting crowd. He didn't see Erin. Turning back he heard Dave say, "Yeah, my little sister hits harder than Jinks."

Cole extended his hand to Dave and pulled him upright. "Come on Dave, let's go home."

Once outside, Cole asked, "What was that all about anyway?"

"Don't know. I was just sitting there minding my own business. I saw Jason come into the gym from the side door but didn't pay much attention. Next thing I know he's in my face jabbering about how he could have thrown better passes than you."

"What?"

"I know. Didn't make much sense to me. I thought he was kidding around. I just looked up at him and joked, 'no man, I've seen your arm.' I even smiled. Then out of nowhere, he punched me."

"He asked me earlier if I wanted some beer he had in the car," Cole said. He thought for a minute. "You know, his speech was a little slurred. I've heard my dad enough. I'll bet the prick was drinking even before the dance."

Dave stopped and grabbed Cole's arm, turning him. He leaned his face close. "Cole, you stay out of this. I'll handle it."

~ * ~

Saturday rolled by in slow motion for Cole. He tried reading but couldn't concentrate. He glanced at the wall clock and his watch repeatedly until noon when he thought it would be safe to call Erin without appearing too anxious.

A female voice answered the phone. "Erin?" he tentatively asked.

"No," the woman said, "but she's right here. Who is this please?"

"Ah... Cole McKenna."

"Just a minute."

Cole felt his face burning as he waited. Erin's lilting voice sounded like music to Cole when she said, "Hi, Cole. What happened last night?"

"Oh, not much. Jason Jinks sucker-punched Dave Thompson for no reason. I think he was drinking."

"Wow. That's crazy."

"I know." A period of silence hung on the line. "Ah, Erin, ah... are we still on for the movie?"

"Oh, sure. I told Dad I explained the rules to you and he said okay, but you'll have to come in and meet him and Mom."

"Okay. Where do you live?"

She gave him her address and Cole wrote it on the same napkin as her number. "The early show starts at seven," he said, "so I'd better come to your house at about six-thirty. That should give us plenty of time to walk to the theater. Is that all right?"

"Sure, that'll be good. See ya then."

"Okay, bye." Cole hung up the phone. The rest of the day inched by even slower than the morning had. In desperation for something to do, Cole even cleaned his room. Mikey followed him around with a look of wonder permanently fixed on his face. Cole showered twice and brushed his teeth three times. Cole's mom smiled most of the day.

Cole knew the street Erin had told him. It was on the other side of town near the high school. An easy ride he was used to. He rode his bike into the plat just off of North Market Street about five blocks from downtown at six-fifteen. He stopped at the beginning of Erin's street and looked at his watch. Too early. He scanned the houses in the development. It looked like about every fifth house was the same design. Most were one story frame construction with attached garages. Judging from the number on the first house on his right, her place would be a couple of blocks further. He waited a few more minutes before riding on.

When Cole saw the right house number, he rode his bike onto the concrete driveway and parked it at the edge under a basketball hoop. As he approached the front door, Cole's nerves jangled. His resolve shed like autumn leaves in a strong wind. He'd have to talk to her parents. She'd be there. They'd grill him. He'd rather fight both Shaw boys at once.

Cole wiped his hands on his pants legs and tried to think what he'd say. How do you do Sir, my name's Cole McKenna. I've come to escort your daughter to the movie. Sure. He stood at the door, finger raised to the button. He couldn't push it.

The door whooshed open and sucked air around him. A large body stood in the doorway above him, legs spread and hands on his hips.

Cole scanned up at the man with trepidation. His brain refused to work. His mouth turned to cotton. He forced himself to look at the man's face.

Officer Tom Bradley's wide grin beamed at him.

Eleven

Cole jerked his head, first to the street, then quickly back to the house. The numbers were right there next to the door. Had he written the wrong address? What the hell's going on?

"So you think you want to date my daughter, huh?" Bradley's smile morphed into a mock scowl.

The same steel gray eyes that had bored into Cole's soul when he was twelve, probed him now. "Daughter? Ahh, no... I mean, I didn't know. You mean...?"

Bradley stepped out grinning, and wrapped a huge arm around Cole's shoulders. "Come on in, Cole. I'll tell you all about it."

The foyer opened into a living room where Erin and a woman, apparently her mother, stood with wide smiles. Erin broke out in laughter. She pointed to Cole. "You should see your face." She giggled.

"Cole, this is my wife, Pam." He swept his hand toward Erin's mother.

"Pam, this is the notorious Mr. Cole McKenna, my young partner in crime fighting."

Cole stood immobile except for his head swiveling back and forth between Mr. Bradley, his wife, and Erin. Finally, he forced his brain into gear and tentatively offered his hand to Mrs. Bradley. "Hi," he muttered.

Taking his hand, Mrs. Bradley said, "I'm pleased to meet you, Cole. Tom and Erin have told me so much about you."

"Me, too," Cole said, just before his brain screamed, stupid, stupid. *'Me too.' God I'm stupid.* He looked at the floor as the heat rose in his face again.

"Come on, Cole," Bradley draped an arm over Cole's shoulder. "Have a seat on the couch. You've got some time yet before the movie."

Cole sat, still trying to clear the embarrassing fog from his mind.

Looking at Bradley, he said, "Erin never told me her last name. I didn't know...I was confused when you opened the door."

Bradley smiled. "When she described the boy she'd met at school, I knew it was you. I told her not to tell you. I wanted to see your reaction. Boy, it was worth the wait." He slapped his leg and let loose a belly laugh.

Cole heard Mrs. Bradley and Erin laughing and snickering from the kitchen. Mr. Bradley leaned in close to Cole and whispered, "I never told Erin you were a thief though." He watched Cole's face for a reaction. "You know that onion thing." He winked then roared with more laughter.

"What?" Erin said as she came into the living room with a bowl of chips.

"Oh, nothing. Cole and I were just talking about our criminal investigation history."

"Yeah, you told me about that." She turned to Cole. "Dad says you did a good job, and that you'd make a good police officer someday."

Cole couldn't think of anything to say. He knew his face must still be red. Finally he said, "Well, they were trying to blame me. I had to do something."

Cole felt relief settle over him when Mr. Bradley changed the subject. "That was some game last night, Cole. Looks like the team will do pretty well this year."

Finally, something he could talk about. "Yes, Sir. Our front line is doing a great job and our defense is strong."

"Next week will be a real test though," Bradley said. "Ashville is also undefeated so far this year."

Cole grimaced. "Yeah, they're tough every year. But Coach Wion told us he has some plans for them."

"Sounds good. Hey, you guys want me to drive you to the movie?"

Cole looked at Erin. She stood. "No, Dad," she said with a look on her face that implied, 'duh'. "We have time to walk, if we leave now."

"Okay." Bradley also got up and extended his hand to Cole. "You watch over her."

"Oh, I will," Cole said.

Cole and Erin strolled the residential streets to the downtown section. The trees were just starting to get some color. Although technically fall, Indian summer had settled over Brockton and the evening was warm. Cole eyed Erin trying not to be obvious. Her honey hair hung naturally to her shoulders under a red head band. The red elastic belt at the top of her short ruffled skirt made her waist appear small enough for Cole to encircle it with both hands, fingers still touching. She wore shiny black leotards with red leg warmers at her ankles. His mind whirled. Man she's pretty.

Cole glanced at his drab Kakis and brown crew neck sweater. She looks like a peacock walking along with one of Grandma's brown chickens.

As they neared the movie theater, Erin asked, "What movie are we going to see?"

Cole wanted to see Full Metal Jacket, but instead said, "I think the Princess Bride might be good." He was pleased he'd managed to say that without his face turning sour.

"Oh, good. I saw the previews and wanted to see that one."

Relaxing in his seat, Cole actually got into the movie and enjoyed it. He was surprised that it had some good action as well as the mushy stuff. Cole rested his right hand on the arm rest trying to figure out a way to let it drop to her hand resting in her lap. During an intense scene, Erin leaned to him and clutched his arm with both hands. After that their hands entwined and stayed that way through the rest of the movie. During one of the action scenes she squeezed his hand. He looked at her. Their eyes locked and he squeezed back. It was difficult to concentrate on the movie after that.

Walking Erin home, still hand in hand, Cole's anxiety built. What do I do? Should I try to kiss her? What would it feel like? What if she doesn't want to? What if her dad comes out? Aaarg.

Erin talked non-stop about school and other girls in her class. Cole didn't hear any of it. His mind remained occupied by more important things. Erin abruptly turned and tugged his arm to follow. Cole shook his head, to clear it, and looked around. She turned onto her driveway. How'd they get here so quick? They climbed the three steps to the small porch. At the door, she stopped and faced him. "Well, thanks, Cole. I really had a good time."

"Me, too." Shifting from one foot to the other, he started to feel the heat rise again, then realized that 'me, too' was perfectly all right in this context.

"Would you like to come in a while?" she asked.

"Ahh, no. I don't think I want to face your dad just yet." He tried a smile.

"Okay, then." She stretched up on tip toes and softly brushed her lips against his. "Good night, Cole. See you in school."

Cole felt his feet trying to float off the ground as a warm flush filled his body. When she turned for the door, he forced his feet to move toward his bike.

~ * ~

At Monday afternoon football practice, Cole was surprised to see Jason Jinks in uniform. Why the hell wasn't he suspended? He'd have to ask the coach after practice. The shrill whistle blast brought activity to a stop and all heads turned to Coach Wion.

"Scrimmage!" The coach yelled. "First string defense." As players shuffled over the dusty practice field to their assigned positions, Wion continued, "Ashville's fullback is averaging six yards a carry and most of those are from off-tackle plunges. So defense, I want you to plug up those four and five, gaps." He turned to the second team. "Offense, run 44 and 45 dive and throw in a 41 trap until the defense can stop them."

Cole took his defensive position at the right corner and Dave set up at the left corner. This should be an easy scrimmage for us, Cole thought. If they run dive plays all day, all we have to do is check the receivers at the line. The middle linemen would do all the heavy work. A part of him was disappointed that he wouldn't get much action, but coach will probably have the offense run some pass plays later on and then we'll have to cover the receivers. That's our primary job, he reminded himself. Maybe he'll have them run some sweeps and we'll get some action then. Yep, this should be an easy day.

The second string offense lined up with Jason Jinks under the center. When the center snapped the ball into his hands, Jinks pivoted and handed it off to Kevin Frock, the second-string fullback. Jinks casually turned back to watch the play unfold just in time to absorb the full impact of Dave's six-foot-four, hundred and ninety pounds ramming him at full speed.

Jinks lay on the ground looking confused and in pain. "What?" Dave said, standing over him. "You weren't expecting that? Oh, sorry, I thought you liked the unexpected." He pointed down at Jinks. "Better get used to it. I'm coming for you on every play, unless you want to go man to man after practice."

Coach Wion yelled, "Thompson." He ran to Dave and grabbed him by the face mask, jerking his head to face him, "What the hell do you think you're doing? You knew the play. What the hell's gotten into you?"

"Dave hung his head and scrunched his face. "Sorry coach. I just got confused."

Wion let go of Dave and just stared at him. "Confused? You've played that position for two years. When have I ever had you blitz?"

"Uhh, never."

"Right," the coach said, "never."

Wion shook his head and walked back to the sideline. "Run it again, he yelled.

Cole looked at Dave with his hands out, palms up and shoulders shrugged, with the silent question.

Dave only grinned back at him.

When the offense lined up, Jinks glanced at Dave as he set up under the center. The ball snapped into his hands and he turned to hand off to the fullback. He let go of the ball before Frock even got to him and fumbled. Jinks turned quickly to the right corner. Dave was boring down on him at full speed. Jinks turned and ran for the sideline and kept going until he disappeared into the locker room.

Cole and the rest of the team stood frozen, absorbed in the drama they'd just witnessed.

Dave only smiled. When red-faced Coach Wion stormed in front of him, Dave said, "I think you'd better get another second-string quarterback, Coach. That one seems to be a coward."

The veins in the coach's neck looked about to explode. "I don't know what the hell you're trying to prove, Thompson, but I'll not have it." He pointed to the locker room. "You're out of here. Hit the showers--now!"

Twelve

The entire team stood gawking at the drama between Dave and the coach. Cole sidled up to the middle linebacker, Matt Jennings, the senior team captain. "Hey, Matt, you got any idea why Jinks is even dressed after that stunt he pulled at the dance?"

"Not really, but I did hear coach say he wanted to get the whole story before he did anything. Now it kinda looks like Dave's screwed it all up."

"Can you talk to the coach about it?"

"Yeah, I was going to anyway. Jason punched Dave for no reason." He grinned, "Hell, I'd have gone after him, too."

"Can I come with you when you talk to him?"

"Sure. Hang around after showers and we'll go to his office."

The rest of the practice was a waste. None of the players could concentrate on their assignments. There was no spark in the team. They missed blocks, missed tackles, and fumbled the ball. Coach Wion flitted around the practice field like Pac Man chewing up players as he arrived at each mistake. His frustrations grew with each play they ran. As the afternoon waned, his foul mood worsened. Finally he blew a shrill blast on his whistle and called out, "Okay, guys, that's enough for today. Hit the showers."

Matt and Cole took their time getting dressed, waiting for the team to clear the locker room. The humidity hung thick enough to form clouds. By the time he dressed, Cole's clothes were damp. They walked the short hall to the coach's office amid the permeating odors of sweaty uniforms and wintergreen analgesic balm. Before arriving at the door, Matt said, "This could be a bad time, Cole. He wasn't happy with this practice today. Hell, I wasn't either."

"Yeah, but I'd like to have my say before he comes down on Dave."

"Okay, but just be ready to back off if he's in a foul mood. You know how intense he can be."

Through the door window they saw Coach Wion bent over some paperwork at his desk. Matt knocked on the door. The coach glanced up from his work, "Come," his voice boomed.

Matt stuck his head between the door and frame. "Coach, can we talk to you for a minute?"

Coach Wion sighed heavily and sat up straight. "Yeah, come on in, Matt." When he saw Cole enter as well, the coach squinted a jaundiced eye at him.

"Coach, as team captain," Matt began, "I wanted to talk to you about Dave and Jason."

"Yeah, I figured that," Wion said. "Not sure I want to discuss it now. And before you start, I want you to know I will not tolerate that kind of behavior."

Cole took a step closer to the desk, "What about Jason's behavior at the dance?"

Coach gave him a glaring look. "Young man, I'll deal with that in due time. It's none of your concern." He turned his accusing stare on Matt, as if to say, 'why is he here?'

Matt turned sharply to Cole, his face grim.

Cole shook his head. He had a lot of respect for Coach Wion, but this attitude confused him. He felt his anger rising. He stepped closer to the desk and said, "But Coach..."

Matt grabbed his arm and said, "Let me talk to the coach." His eyes told Cole to shut up. He lifted his chin toward the door.

Cole stood his ground until Matt's glare got the message across. He reluctantly turned to the door and left.

Cole sat on a locker-room bench waiting for Matt to come out of the office. Despite the variety of odors and echoing tile walls, Cole loved locker rooms. They made him feel like he belonged. When Matt finally showed up, he said nothing but motioned for Cole to follow him out of the building.

Walking toward the parking lot, Matt said, "Something weird's going on, Cole. The coach is acting different. I think he's getting pressure from someplace."

Cole curled his lip and frowned. "What kind of pressure? About what?"

"Don't know. He's not acting like himself today."

Cole thought it over. Something's not right. Jason should have been suspended for what he did at the dance. Yet here he was at practice like nothing happened. Then the coach gets mad at Dave. "What did he say about Dave?"

"He's going to bench him for one game, provided he doesn't pull another stunt like he did in practice today. He wanted to do more than that but I talked him out of it."

"Oh, crap. That's not right. Dave's too important to the team. We've got Ashville next week."

"I know, but you saw what happened. Coach gave him a direct order not to blitz and Dave did it anyway. Coach can't let that happen. We're lucky it's only for one game."

Cole tightened his jaw and hung his head. *Matt was right. What the hell was Dave thinking?*

You know he usually lets the team decide disciplinary actions," Matt continued, "but this was a direct slap to the coach."

"Yeah," Cole acknowledged. "But what's he gonna do about Jason sucker-punching Dave?"

"I don't know." He pursed his lips and raised his eyebrows, then winked at Cole. "Maybe let the team handle that one."

~ * ~

Coach Wion cradled his head in both hands, elbows propped on his desk. Damn, he knew things were going way too smoothly this year. Now he was at risk of the team falling apart. All because some hot-head knee-jerk reactions. He sat up straight when the phone jingled.

"Wion," he growled into the phone.

"Coach, this is Superintendent Stubbs. I just heard one of your players assaulted another one. Is that true?"

Wion took a deep breath. Stubbs' spies must be working overtime. Of course, almost everyone at the dance had witnessed Jinks' assault. "Yes, Sir, that's true but I'm dealing with it."

"That's good, Coach. We cannot tolerate bullying in our school. Students must understand what it means to act as civilized human beings."

"I know, Sir. I'll make sure they both understand the consequences of their acts, and the team will decide their punishment."

"Both?" Mr. Stubbs said. "I hardly think it's necessary to include Jason, when the colored boy initiated the assault."

"Colored boy?" Wion shouted into the phone before thinking. *Where in the hell has this fool been for the past three decades?* He forced himself to relax. "Sir, I don't know what you've heard, but let me clarify a few things for you."

"I'm not sure I appreciate your attitude, Coach."

Wion felt the veins in his neck pounding as if about to explode. "Sir, perhaps you don't know all the facts..."

"I certainly understand we cannot tolerate bullying."

"Mr. Stubbs, listen to me." Wion pinched the bridge of his nose to keep from shouting again. "Jason Jinks sucker-punched Dave at the school dance Friday. Out of the blue, he just walked up and hit him. Did you know about that?"

A long silence hung on the phone, before Stubbs said, "Ah, no, I didn't. But I was told that today at practice the ... uh... Thompson boy, attacked Jason Jinks."

How in hell had he heard about that so quickly? "I'd hardly call it an attack. He tackled him and disobeyed my orders. That's the only reason Dave's in trouble. Jason is the one I'm worried about. I'm afraid if I let the team dish out the punishment, like I usually do, they'll vote to kick him off the team."

"Kick him off? But his father..."

"I know his dad's the president of the booster club. I don't need reminding of that."

"They buy a lot of equipment and supplies for all our sports teams."

"I know, I know. That's what I'm wrestling with right now."

"Coach, could today's attack have been deliberate? That might make it an even exchange." There was a pleading tone in the voice.

"Deliberate." Wion's voice rose again. "Of course it was deliberate. Hell, this is football. It's a rough sport. The kid got tackled. No big deal. Then he ran away like a coward. Now, that is a big deal."

The silent receiver burned Wion's ear as he waited for a response from his boss. His brain, however, remained occupied with his team problem.

"Well," Mr. Stubbs said. "I can see you have a conundrum on your hands. Just try to settle this matter in a way that's good for the school." Wion understood the unspoken threat.

"I do not envy your position," Mr. Stubbs concluded.

"Me either," Wion muttered replacing the phone on its cradle.

Thirteen

Cole stopped by Dave's house on his way home from practice. The bike ride and late afternoon warm fall heat brought a trickle of perspiration to his forehead. He put down the kickstand just inside the picket fence and three big strides put him on Dave's front porch.

Dave had a wide grin pasted on his face when he opened the front door. "Hey Cole, what's up?"

Cole shook his head. "Just trying to figure out what got into you today at practice. Man, you must be crazy."

"Yeah, I guess so." He held his index finger to his lips. "Come on in. Want a Coke?"

"Sure." Cole followed Dave into the kitchen. At the stove, stirring something in a large cast iron skillet, Dave's mother turned to greet him. "Hello, young Cole, how you doing?"

"I'm good, Mrs. T. Just dropped by to see if Dave can help with my homework."

"You staying for supper?" She held up a crispy golden brown chicken leg for Cole to see.

"No thank you, Ma'am. Mom will expect me soon, but it sure smells good."

She gave him a warm smile before turning back to the skillet.

Dave grabbed two Cokes from the refrigerator and handed one to Cole, nodding for him to follow. Once inside Dave's bedroom, Cole hissed, "What the hell were you trying to prove today?"

Dave stared at him for a moment. "Just that Jinks is a coward. Guess I did, huh?"

"Well, yeah," Cole acknowledged. "But you sure pissed off Coach."

"He'll get over it."

"Maybe so, but he'll probably bench you for a game or two."

"Well, I need the rest."

"You butt! This ain't funny. It's serious Dave. We need you in the lineup."

"Chill, man. I'll be back. It's only a game or two."

"But Why, Dave?"

Dave took a deep breath. "I don't know..." he shuffled around, "I'm kinda in the minority around school, and... I just couldn't let him punch me and get away with it. Probably shouldn't have done it a practice, but I couldn't control myself."

Cole twisted his face and shook his head. "Well, Jason deserved worse than what he got, but now you're the one who has to pay. It's not fair, Dave."

Dave said, "Let it go, man. I'll be okay."

Cole eyed him a moment longer then shook it off. "Okay, just be an ass then." He lightly punched Dave's upper arm.

Dave laughed and grabbed Cole in a headlock.

"Mrs. T," Cole yelled. "Dave's beating me up again." The boys staggered around the room until Cole hooked a leg behind Dave and pulled them both to the floor with a thud.

"You two better knock it off before I come in there and show you what a real beating is," Mrs. T's deep melodic voice echoed down the hall. They laughed as they continued to roll around on the floor.

~ * ~

That evening, sitting at the antique oak claw-foot table picking at his food, Bob Wion wrestled with his problems. Bad enough to have to worry about what's going on with Jason, but on top of that, all the pressure from Stubbs, and now, probably the boosters. Don't need this crap.

"What's going on, Bob?" his wife, Leah asked. "You've been preoccupied all evening. Something's bothering you. What is it?"

Wion sighed, then outlined the situation between Dave and Jason adding the details of the superintendent's phone call. "Damn it. Stubbs was pretty clear that I'd better solve this problem and keep the support of the boosters." He looked up at Leah, his face grim. "I could get fired over this. Damn it." He slammed an open hand on the table. "I don't do community relations. I'm here to win football games." Elbows on the table, he rested his head between his hands.

Leah touched his shoulder until he looked up. She stared at him as if he had been a naughty boy and said, "Are you a good coach, Bob?"

"Huh? What the hell does that have to do with anything?"

"Are you?" Her head remained tilted down with that accusing look.

"Well, yeah, I guess so, but--"

"I know you, Bob," Leah interrupted. "If you do what is good for your job instead of what's right, you'll no longer be a good coach." She paused to let her words sink in. "We came here looking for a job. So if you get fired because of politics you wouldn't want to be here anyway. You've established a good record as coach so you wouldn't have any trouble finding another job." She smiled. "Hell, I'd even go with you."

Wion shook his head. "Boy, you cut right to the chase, don't you?"

"You taught me." A satisfied grin lit her face.

Bob stood and hugged his wife. He tucked her under his right shoulder and turned for the living room. Walking hip to hip he leaned down and kissed her forehead. "You're my rock, Darlin'."

~ * ~

By Wednesday, Wion knew he couldn't wait any longer for a decision. Jason Jinks hadn't been to school for two days and missed today's practice. He'd delve into Jason's situation later. The coach stood blocking the locker room door letting his senses absorb the sights, sounds and scents of his beloved world. The jokes, jibes, locker doors slamming, and thwacking pads into place, were music to him. Young men having fun at something they loved as much as he did. He inhaled deeply. God I love the smell of a locker room.

While the team dressed, he called out, "Team meeting before we go out."

The boys shuffled around the room still adjusting pads. The din quieted as they gathered around the coach.

"Boys we've got some issues to straighten out. First thing first-- Dave, you know the other day you disobeyed my direct order. For that, and only that," he paused and looked directly at Dave, "You'll ride the bench Friday night."

Dave nodded and hung his head.

"Now," the coach continued, "the other matter is a team deportment issue, and therefore a team decision. You all know what happened at the dance last Friday. I'm going to leave you here to discuss Jason's actions and what should be done about it. You vote as a team and decide what, if any, discipline is needed. Matt," he looked at the captain, "you report to me what the decision is and that's the end of it. Dave, you don't have a vote."

Coach Wion left the locker room.

When the team swarmed from the locker room toward the practice field to start calisthenics, Wion went back in and motioned for Matt to come to his office.

"Well, Matt, what's the verdict?"

Matt grimaced. "Coach, we talked about a lot more than just the fight at the dance. I didn't know about it all but some of the other guys said Jason has been acting really strange ever since two-a-days. Some even thought he started being all weird last year after football season."

"Weird, how?"

"Not sure, Coach, just different--kinda withdrawn. Last year, he was okay--you know, looking forward to being quarterback his senior year. Then Cole developed so well and beat him out. I think that really bothered him. Anyway, he's been like a loner since then. Some of the players used to be close to him but they said he doesn't hang with them anymore. He's missed some school lately too."

Wion leaned back in his chair, fingers steepled. After a moment, he said, "So what'd the guys decide?"

"We've got a good team here, Coach and we want to keep it that way. We don't need no distractions. It was unanimous. We voted to kick him off the team."

Fourteen

Coach Wion paced himself as he walked from his office to the Superintendent's. He had anticipated the call, but the timing couldn't have been worse. He had far better things to do on a Friday afternoon, like prepare for the game against Ashville. He didn't relish the confrontation, but he'd done his research and set his mind. He would stand his ground.

"Mr. Wion, are you sure you want to do this?" Mr. Stubbs asked, without any preamble.

Bob decided to play teenager and not give him the satisfaction of thinking this was the most important topic of his day. "Do what, Mr. Stubbs?'

"Don't play games with me, Bob. You know what I'm talking about. Now, why did you suspend Jason Jinks from the team?"

"I didn't. The team did."

"What?" Stubbs raised his voice and half stood from his chair.

Bob held his hand up. "We have a rule, Mr. Stubbs. Anything to do with team deportment, they vote on the discipline."

"That's the dumbest thing I've ever heard. You can't let a bunch of teenagers run your football team."

"Oh, they don't run it. They just vote on disciplinary matters."

"Well you just veto that vote."

"I can't do that Mr. Stubbs."

"And why not?"

"Mostly because I agree with it."

Stubbs' mouth fell open. He sat heavily back into his chair. "Coach, I think you're committing career suicide here. Mr. Jinks is a very influential member of this community. He was livid when he came to see me this morning, and he demanded reinstatement and an apology."

"Can't see where he has any right to demand anything. If you want to fire me, that's your prerogative, but that won't get Jason back on the team. And it sure won't get any apology."

"What?" Stubbs raised his voice again. "I'll not put up with... You're way out of line here coach."

Bob pulled a manila folder from his clipboard and laid it on the desk. "I did some checking. Jason has missed six days of school already this quarter. He can't possibly play football. And he's legitimately failing three subjects so far. By school policy, he won't be eligible for sports or any extra-curricular activities after this quarter anyway."

Stubbs sank into his oversized chair. "What if he brings the grades up?" he countered.

"Something's going on with that young man, Mr. Stubbs. He won't have time to bring the grades up. He has a zero in two of the classes he's failing." Bob leaned forward and put both hands on Stubbs' desk. "Look, Jason's been one of my players for three years and I'm concerned about him. You better believe I'm going to find out what his problem is. It might take some time, but I'll get to the bottom of this."

"Have you talked to Jason?"

"Well of course I have. Why do you think his dad came to see you?" Bob waved the question off. "To tell the truth, I think he was actually relieved when I told him the team had voted to boot him. That way he could tell his dad and lay the blame on someone else. I guess that'd be me."

Stubbs closed his eyes. One hand went to his forehead. "What in the world am I going to tell Mr. Jinks? He was really mad this morning. He threatened to withhold the booster support."

"Tell him the truth. He should be more concerned about his son failing than he is with him not playing football."

Stubbs looked up. "He'll want your job, Coach."

Bob nodded. "You know, most of the other members of the boosters have kids on the team and it was their kids that voted him off. And those parents seem pretty happy with our program lately."

"You do know that Jinks owns the creamery in town and some of the fathers work for him?" Stubbs interjected.

"I do." Bob squared his shoulders. "I coach football. Most of the dads want a winning team. I remember when I gave my little inaugural speech seven years ago, about building character and sportsmanship in their boys. Someone yelled out, 'Bullshit. You better win football games.' There was a lot of applause to that comment. I think we've done that. We've had some pretty good years since then. So I don't think they'll all go along with him."

"It's more than winning football games to Jinks." Stubbs said.

"I know. And if the pressure gets to hot... Well then the ball will be in your court. I can't control that. You might want to call some of the other booster members and feel them out. Try to remember Mr. Stubbs, it's you and the school board who decides who to hire and fire, not the boosters."

Stubbs glared at him.

~ * ~

Brockton suffered their first loss of the season to Ashville that evening, twenty-seven to twenty-one. Dave's replacement at wide receiver dropped four of Cole's perfect passes. On defense, once Ashville found they could sweep their right side, they pounded out yardage and two touchdowns. When Coach Wion changed Cole to that side, It didn't take Ashville long to run the other end for more yardage and another touchdown. Now, unless Ashville lost to another school, Brockton had no chance at winning the league championship.

Cole attended the school dance that night, but he and the rest of the team sat huddled at a table, still stewing over the coach's locker room words. 'Losing was nothing to be ashamed of, letting the other beat them was.' Their sullen mood spread throughout the gym. No one approached the table. Most of the team left before the dance ended. When Mr. Ervin announced the final dance of the evening, the remaining team members rose and shuffled toward the exits like zombies.

Cole wound his way to Erin's table and held out his hand to her.

"You finally noticed I was here, huh?" she said.

"Sorry," Cole mumbled. *She just don't get it. This was an important game and we blew it.* "You want to dance or not?"

She shoved her chair back as she stood. Erin glared at him before saying, "Fine."

She grabbed his hand and marched to the dance floor. They swayed woodenly to the music a short while. *Man, nothing's going right tonight.* Cole knew his attitude was wrong, but she would never understand. How could she? His thoughts were interrupted when Erin stepped on his foot. They both stumbled. They stopped dancing and looked into each other's eyes. Spontaneous laugher erupted and they melted together in a forgiving hug. Relaxing against each other, they continued to dance. At the end of the song Erin said, "I'm sorry. I know you're bummed."

"No," Cole said. "I'm the one who's sorry. I shouldn't have ignored you and I'm a butt head. Still friends?"

She pecked him on the cheek. "It'll take more than that to get rid of me."

They left the gymnasium together and walked hand in hand to Erin's house. After a long silence, Erin said, Want to talk about it?"

"No, you wouldn't understand."

"Well, excuse me for being a girl." Her voice registered her anger. ""A girl who plays basketball, I might add. We've lost important games too."

Cole stopped and held on to her hand when she tried to walk off. "Erin," he pleaded. "I'm sorry." He hung his head. "I'm such a jerk."

She glared at him a moment. "Yep."

"I really am sorry," he said, putting his arm around her shoulder as they continued walking.

Standing on her front porch, Erin grabbed his hands and said, "Boy, I hope you guys don't lose any more games. It makes you a different person."

"Sorry, I just don't like to lose. The sad thing is, we shouldn't have lost tonight" His voice rose. "It's all so stupid."

"What's stupid?" Mr. Bradley said when he opened the door.

"Oh, nothing," Cole said, quickly looking away. The silence hung heavy while Cole tried to think of a way out of this discussion.

Erin broke the awkward silence. "Well, good night, Cole."

"Yeah," he tried to sound upbeat but knew he had failed. "Good night."

When Erin turned for the door, Bradley said, "Cole, can I talk to you a minute?"

Cole's heart sank and his shoulders sagged. He couldn't help releasing a sigh. The last thing he needed now was a lecture from a girl's father. But this was Officer Bradley, his hero. "Yeah, I guess so."

"Let's have a seat." He draped a massive arm over Cole's shoulders and guided him to the porch swing. "Can't blame you for being upset. That was a tough one to lose, and losing ain't much fun, is it?"

Cole hung his head. "No, Sir."

"The team sure didn't seem to play like they usually do tonight. You got any idea what the problem was?"

Oh man, I don't need this. We lost. That's what happened. He shuffled around on the wooden slats. "I don't know. We just lost focus, I guess. That's what the coach said anyway. We couldn't get into any rhythm."

"Why not?" Bradley pressed, lifting Cole's chin to look him in the eyes.

Cole felt like Officer Bradley was interrogating him. He didn't want to get into it, but he didn't want to dis Bradley either. He took a deep breath and exhaled. When he spoke, all the frustration of the past few days poured out. "Aw heck, I don't know. Probably all the mess with Dave and Jason Jinks. Dave had to sit the bench, Jason was voted off the team, and Matt told us he heard the coach might lose his job." Cole leaned forward and dropped his head into his hands.

"Erin told me about the Jinks boy but I didn't know the coach was catching flack over it."

"Yeah, and it's not even his fault. We voted him off."

Bradley thought for a moment. "Do you know what's going on with Jinks?"

Cole looked up. His eyes squinted and head cocked to one side. "What do you mean?"

"Well I heard about the fight last Friday. Didn't seem like something a teammate would do to another. I just wondered if you knew anything else that might have led up to it. It also doesn't seem like a good enough reason to kick someone off the team either."

Cole squinted his eyes in thought. "Yeah, it seemed harsh to me and Dave too. Some of the seniors said Jason had been complaining all year about the way the coach ran the team and they thought he'd been acting strange since school started. So there was more to it than just the fight. They thought he was dragging the team down."

"Okay, Cole," he put both hands on Cole's shoulders and turned him "This is between you and me, okay?" He waited for Cole's nod.. "I've been getting some information about certain things going on at the high school and that's why I wanted to talk to you. Jason Jinks' name has come up. Can you keep your eyes and ears open and let me know anything you find out about him?"

Cole jerked to attention. "Things? What kind of things?"

Bradley looked around. "I don't want to accuse anybody yet, but there's talk about drugs at school."

"Drugs?" Cole started to sit up, then eased back. "I've always heard talk about some kids doing pot, but I always thought it was just to make them seem tough."

"And this could be nothing more than that, Cole. But it could also involve something much more serious. All I want you to do is keep your eyes and ears open and let me know if you hear of anything involving drugs, especially drugs other than pot. We don't want that kind of activity in our town. Okay?"

"No, Sir," Cole said. His mind filled with excitement. Bradley needed his help. No longer depressed by thoughts of losing a football game, Cole's mind sprang into action. He would be involved in another investigation with Bradley.

Fifteen

Walking home, Cole's mind buzzed with wild plans to investigate the school drug cartel. He envisioned an organized mafia group enticing young children into the world of drugs, like he'd seen on big city TV shows. Maybe Jason Jinks had been lured into addiction and couldn't be responsible for his actions. He'd talk to Jason tomorrow and try to help him. No, he couldn't do that, it would tip his hand. He was undercover now. He'd pay more attention to the various groups at school. He'd follow Jason like he had the Shaw brothers and find his source of drugs, then he'd call Bradley and the troops in for the bust. Sure, Bradley had told him not to do anything except keep his eyes and ears open, but maybe he could solve this case.

By the time he got home, he had worked himself into the role of Sonny Crockett. He pictured Dave as Rico Tubbs. Together they would be Brockton Vice.

Cole walked through the back door and froze. His mother sat waiting at the kitchen table. What's she doing up? She usually rose early for work. "Hi, Cole," she said. "I saw the game." She sipped coffee from her cup. "I'm sorry you lost. You must feel terrible. How did the dance go?" Cole furrowed his brow. His mother's voice sounded flat.

"Not much better than the game." He hung his head. "I was in a funk, Mom. I think Erin's mad at me... What are you still doing up anyway? Don't you have to work tomorrow?

"No Honey, I'm afraid not."

Cole's head jerked up. Her shoulders sagged and her face wore a forlorn expression. "Oh, Mom, what happened? Did you lose your job?" Cole's heart fluttered. He started around the table.

"Kinda," she said, then she looked up at Cole and let a slow smile brighten her face.

Cole eased into a chair across the table from his mom. "What?"

Her smile broadened and her eyes sparkled. "Today, Mr. Peters promoted me to manager of the restaurant." Her face continued to beam. "And, I get a big raise." Her arms shot over her head. "Mr. Peters was so nice. He complimented me about my work and loyalty and everything. I'll have regular hours and weekends off." Her voice reflected her excitement.

Cole sucked in a deep breath. He stood and ran around the table, pulled his mother from the chair and swung her around. "That's great, Mom. You deserve it."

"And," she continued, "now we can move out of this dump and into a real home. I've been thinking about it all day."

Cole squeezed her tighter. "Wow, that would be great. Did you tell Mikey?"

"Yes. Your brother wasn't real excited about it though. He wants to stay with his friends, but he'll get used to the idea."

"When can we move?"

"The sooner the better. We'll start looking tomorrow. We'll still have to rent, but it'll be a house--not..." she waved her arm around the room, "this."

Cole tossed and turned in bed, that night. His mind refused to relax. So much had happened in one day. They lost their first game, the coach might be fired, Erin was probably mad at him, Officer Bradley wanted him to help with an investigation, and they could move out of the projects. On top of all that, his sixteenth birthday would soon be here and he could get his driver's license.

~ * ~

Cole and Mikey sat on the couch with their mom between. They pointed and talked about the different neighborhoods as she circled 'for rent' ads in the paper. After she made several phone calls, they were ready to visit the circled properties.

When their car rolled to a stop at the curb in front of the fourth house on their list, Cole turned to Mikey in the back seat. They shared a grin before swiveled back to stare open-mouthed as the house.

Cole seized the door handle and turned to his mother. "Can we really afford a place like this, Mom?"

"We'll see, Hon. We have to look at it first."

A car pulled into the driveway and the driver turned off the engine.

"Aw, somebody already lives here." Cole's shoulders sagged.

"That's the owner," his mother said. "He said he'd meet us here so we could look it over."

They exited the car and approached the man standing in the driveway. While their mom talked to the man, Cole and Mikey gawked at the house and neighborhood. The small frame house in an established plat near the high school seemed perfect to Cole. Its location on the other side of town, far from the projects, made the house and neighborhood all the more appealing.

The muted yellow vinyl siding appeared to be brand new. In the small front yard a medium sized maple tree still held some colorful leaves. The low bushes along the front of the house were neatly trimmed. A flower bed lined the area between the front walk and the driveway. Above the single-car, unattached garage, a basketball hoop and net beckoned the boys, as they followed the owner and their mom up the walk.

Inside, they stood and gazed around the living room. A large picture window occupied the wall to the left of the front door. Through an open archway, they could see part of the kitchen and a real dining room. An air conditioning unit took up the bottom half of an oversized kitchen window.

Mikey and Cole ran down the central hallway. There were three bedrooms and two bathrooms. The floors were covered with wall-to-wall carpet. No more cold linoleum over cement floors. Cole and Mikey flitted from room to room like it was Christmas, bickering about which room they wanted. With no furniture to block their movements, the space seemed as big as the school gym to Cole.

While Mom talked with the owner, Cole and Mikey hustled outside to the fenced-in back yard. They sprinted toward a small shed in the far corner. A grassless space next to the shed, and parallel to the fence, could be an old garden, now high with weeds. Inside the unlocked shed, a few garden tools hung on pegs and a gasoline powered lawn mower and a gas can rested in the middle. . "You have to mow the grass, and I get to tend the garden." Cole teased Mikey.

"Nunt-huh. I get to do a garden and you mow grass."

Cole wrapped his arm around Mikey's shoulders. "Okay, little Bro, then you get to do dishes every night and I'll mow."

"Mom," Mikey yelled, running into the house.

"Can we live here, Mom?" Mikey asked repeatedly. Cole crossed his fingers.

When Cole saw his mother take out her checkbook and start writing a check, he and Mikey both bent and repeatedly arm pumped.

Mrs. McKenna paid the deposit money and signed a lease. Cole shook hands with the owner before heading toward their ancient Ford

Fairlane. "Can I drive home, Mom? I need some practice on this side of town, if I'm going to pass the drivers exam."

"Sure." She handed him the keys. "But be extra careful, we have Mikey with us."

During the drive to the projects, Mikey babbled into Cole's ear about their new house the entire time.

~ * ~

Cole and his family were overwhelmed with packing boxes and getting ready for the move. Wednesday, after football practice, Cole managed to talk a few of his teammates into helping with the move. When they arrived, Bradley and Mr. Lutz were already hauling a couch out to a large trailer Mr. Lutz had brought from his farm.

"Hi, guys," Officer Bradley called as they walked by.

"You old timers were supposed to leave the heavy work for us." Cole jabbed.

"Here, take my end then," Mr. Lutz said.

Cole laughed and waved over his shoulder, as he and his teammates kept on walking. In less than two hours they had loaded everything into the trailer and headed for the new house.

When most of the belongings had been moved into the house, the teammates, except for Dave, drifted off to their own homes.

"See ya next summer, Cole," Mr. Lutz said, as he headed for his pickup and trailer.

"Next summer," Cole called after him, "I bale for free, Mr. Lutz,"

"I might hold you to that," Mr. Lutz said as he climbed into the truck.

Bradley stood on the sidewalk next to Cole. "I'm really happy for you, Cole. And your mom looks so pleased."

"She is. Thank you for helping. Mom's so relieved to be away from the projects. She thinks it'll be good for Mikey, too." They stood and watched Mr. Lutz drive away.

After a moment, Bradley said, "Any news from school?" He winked at Cole.

Cole lowered his voice and his head, "With all that's happened lately, I haven't had much time to check into that... other thing."

"That's all right. I understand. Just keep your eyes and ears open."

"I will."

"Okay, I'd better get home. Pam'll have dinner waiting."

"Thanks again."

"You're welcome."

"Hey, Cole," Dave called from the front porch. "You gonna help out in here? My mom and dad are coming to get me soon, and if you want this cheap labor, you'd better help."

Cole and Dave assembled beds while Mikey and his mom unpacked boxes. At seven o'clock the front doorbell rang. Cole and Mikey raced for the door--their first caller.

Cole got to the door before the others and jerked it open. He was momentarily disappointed. Not a new neighbor. Then he beamed at Mr. and Mrs. Thompson standing on the concrete stoop. "Hi, come on in." Dave's parents each held a large picnic basket.

"Thought you all might be hungry after the move," Mrs. T said, holding up her basket.

Cole held the door open as they entered. Mrs. T looked around the living room and into the kitchen. "My, my, Sharon," she called. "You pretty much have this place together in one short afternoon."

Cole's mom said, "Not quite yet, Mary," as she came from the kitchen, wiping her hands. "We'll have to hang sheets at the windows for tonight. I'll do curtains later. When I'm more familiar with the place, we'll get it organized." She eyed the picnic baskets. "In our rush, I didn't even think about eating. You're a lifesaver, Mary. Come on in the kitchen."

Cole and Dave rooted through boxes until they found Cole's basketball. "Come on, Dad," Dave called, as they ran by the couch where Mr. T sat. "I'll show you how to slam dunk."

Shifting his huge frame from the couch, Mr. T said, "Boy, I been dunking basketballs since I was twelve." He wrapped his massive arms around Dave and Cole's necks and lightly banged their heads together. The guys headed to the driveway for some hoops while the women set about preparing a meal. "Make it short," Mrs. T called after them.

~ * ~

After the Thompsons left, Cole, Mikey, and their mom sat talking excitedly about their new home, as the television droned in the background. Sitting in quiet reflection for a moment, Cole said, "Sure was nice of everyone to help us move."

"Yes it was." His mom put her arm around his shoulders. "I was so sorry to hear about Ben, though."

Cole perked up. "What about Mr. T?"

"Didn't Dave tell you? He lost his job."

Cole jumped to his feet. "That's not fair."

"I know, hon, but sometimes things like that happen."

"You don't understand, Mom. He works at the creamery, and Mr. Jinks runs the creamery. He was probably fired because of the fight Dave had with Jason."

Sixteen

The football team was back on track. They won the next two games handily. But since they practiced every day after school, Cole had little opportunity to check on Jason's activities. Being a senior meant Jason's class schedule was far different from Cole's, and their paths didn't cross during the school day. Jason hadn't attended the dances on either Friday night.

That Saturday, a combination of boredom and curiosity got the better of Cole. He decided to ride his bike past Jason's house. Jason lived in a gated community at the edge of Brockton, less than two miles from Cole's new home. Several elegant houses occupied the north shore of a small lake, while the south shore was open to the public. Cole and Dave had fished the lake a few times. He pedaled on by the open gate to the private street. If he rode into the cul-de-sac, Jason might spot him or the neighbors could report him. He continued on to the public side of the lake and took up position at a picnic table near the edge of a stand of trees. Ducks and geese scurried around his feet, looking for a scrap of bread.

Cole hoped to spot cars coming and going at Jason's. He planned to write the descriptions and license plate numbers so Bradley could check them. The binoculars he'd brought along for his stakeout were powerful enough to pull in the rear of Jason's house, but not to detect any movement inside. And the house blocked his view to the front, where any cars would be. *Some smart detective I am.* He blew out a frustrated breath. *Great view of an empty back yard and nothing else.* An hour later the cold convinced him his plan had done little more than waste a good chunk of his Saturday.

How could he get any information for Bradley? He'd tried following Jason one other time, but his bicycle couldn't keep up with Jason's car. He thought about his dilemma while riding home. Maybe he should hone in on anyone hanging around the halls and lunch room with Jason. Maybe they could lead him to the drug dealer, or maybe one of them is the dealer.

After supper, Cole rode to Erin's house, much closer now since he lived on the east side of town. She must have seen him park his bike in the driveway, because she opened the door before he stepped onto the porch. "Hi, Cole. What's up?"

"Not much. Just wanted to drop by, maybe talk a little." Even though they'd gone to the Friday dances, there still seemed to be some tension between them. "Is your dad home?"

"Cole!" she stamped her foot on the porch. "You're impossible." She turned to go back in the house.

"What?" Cole said, grabbing the door.

She stopped and glared at him, breathing heavily. "I think you're more interested in Dad than me."

"Huh?" Cole's brows furrowed. "That's crazy. I just wanted to know if he's home." Sure, he wanted to talk to Bradley for some tips on how to proceed with the investigation, but he wanted to see Erin as well.

"Yeah, well every time you've been here lately, you spend more time with him, than me."

"No I don't, Erin. That's silly."

"Silly!" Her face told Cole he wasn't helping himself by talking. The next instant, he didn't have to worry about what he'd say next. The door slammed in his face.

~ * ~

Cole rushed to the phone as soon as he entered his home, and dialed Erin's number. Mrs. Bradley answered.

"Oh, hi, Mrs. Bradley, it's Cole. May I speak with Erin?" She didn't answer for a moment. A lump worked its way into Cole's throat. *What's going on? Is she mad, too*? "Just a minute," Mrs. Bradley said. "I'll see if she's available."

Available! Her voice sounded so cold.

"What do you want now?" Erin's sharp voice cut into his heart.

"Erin, I'm sorry. I don't know why I'm sorry, but I must have said something to upset you, and I'm sorry."

"Yes, you are!" Cole jerked the receiver from his ear when a click, loud enough to be a gunshot, ended their connection.

~ * ~

After practice on Monday, Cole rode from the stadium parking lot and turned onto Brandt Street toward home. A police cruiser sat idling just beyond the corner. Steamy exhaust billowed from the tail pipe. As he pulled alongside, Officer Bradley, sitting at the steering wheel, waved him down. "Get in, Cole. It's cold out there."

Cole moved his bike to the sidewalk and parked it. Hopping in the front seat, he said, "Hey, Officer Bradley, what's up?"

"Nothing much, I just wanted to have a little talk with you."

"I've tried to get some info for you about Jinks, but I haven't found out anything, yet."

"That's okay, but that's not what I wanted to talk to you about."

"What then?"

"Erin."

Uh oh. Now I've got him mad at me, and I still don't know why. "What about... Erin?" he choked out.

Bradley sucked in a long breath. "Look, Cole, I know your dad isn't around for the usual man-to-man talk, so I guess I have to play both roles." He turned in his seat to face Cole. "This is difficult for me. You should know how much I care about you, but Erin's my little girl and I don't want to see her hurt."

Cole jerked. "I would never..."

"I know, Cole. That's not what I mean. You're both young. Don't get me wrong. I approve of her dating you. She has to develop those skills in her youth. So do you, But..."

Cole's brows pinched together. What in the world is he talking about? "But I..."

"I know. Now just listen. This is hard enough. She's more emotionally involved than I had anticipated. I just thought you two would be friends."

"We are."

Bradley looked sternly at Cole. "Just shut up a minute and I'll try to explain. If you two were in college, I might even encourage her to develop deep feelings for you. That's how much respect I have for you. But... you're not. You're both very young and have a lot of life's lessons to learn. The only way you're going to learn them is to date other people so you'll both have a better grip on what you want." He paused, pulling in another deep breath and exhaled.

"You mean I can't see Erin anymore?" Cole's shoulders sagged and his face pinched.

"Of course I don't mean that. I just want you both to take a step back and maybe date other people as well. You've got all the time in the world."

The silence inside the cruiser hung ominously. Cole tried to absorb what Mr. Bradley had said, but not much of it made sense to him. Am

I not good enough for his daughter? No, Mr. Bradley had even encouraged him. Did she put him up to this?

"Cole," Bradley finally said, "I dated Erin's mom through most of high school. We must have fought and broke up at least a dozen times back then. When she went away to college we both dated other people. We matured. Those experiences with others taught us that no one else was right for us. When we got back together, we knew it was right. Does that make any sense to you?"

Cole hesitated. "Yeah, I guess so," then added, "but we're not doing anything..."

A smile played at Bradley's mouth. "I didn't think anything like that, Cole. I know you both well enough for that." His face turned serious again. "But I also know how it feels to have hormones racing through your body. Just so you know--you will be tempted. Don't kid yourself."

Cole hung his head. He had been having those thoughts a lot lately.

"Did you tell Erin all this?"

"Yes, and I'm glad to see you're not reacting the same way. Tells me even more about you."

Confused again, Cole said. "What?"

"She ran crying to her room. At least she's mad at me now--not you."

Seventeen

Cole trudged through his front door, past the kitchen and the enticing aroma of frying pork chops. He slogged straight to his room and flopped on the bed. He pressed his fingertips to his eyes, trying to rub out the confusion of the past two days. He replayed snippets of the scene at Erin's door in his mind. *What the heck did I do wrong?* His mind flipped to her dad. The blank view of the white ceiling acted as a movie screen. He visualized himself spread eagle against the side of Officer Bradley's cruiser with the enraged officer pointing his gun at his back. He shook his head to erase the vision. *Okay, it wasn't that bad, but what was that talk all about?* The more he agonized over it, the more confused he became.

"Cole!" his mother's voice rang down the hall.

"What?" he yelled back.

"That's the third time I've called you to dinner. Are you deaf?"

Poking his head around the corner of the door, Cole said, "Sorry, Mom, I didn't hear you. But I'm not hungry right now."

"What?" She stepped from the kitchen and looked at him. "Not hungry? That's a new one. Did you have trouble at practice?

"No."

"Flunk a test?"

"No."

His mother walked the hallway toward him. "What's going on, Cole?" She looked squinty-eyed at him.

He sighed, "I don't know, Mom. Erin got mad at me and her dad thinks we should break up."

Her eyes widened. "Why? Did you..."

"No, Mom. I didn't do anything." He rushed through an explanation of his last conversation with Erin. "Why can't girls be more like guys? We can do or say anything to each other and nobody gets offended. Are all girls like that?"

His mother didn't respond for a moment. Then she wrapped her arms around him. "Honey, boys and girls are different, and they perceive things differently." She sighed. "This could take a long time." She took a deep breath. "I guess it's about time we talked about some things." She paused. But I have an idea. I've got a new book I think you should read before we do."

"Mom," He sighed as his shoulders drooped. "Read a book?"

"Actually, I think you might enjoy it. It's called Men are from Mars, Women are from Venus."

"Oh, come on, science fiction?"

She laughed. "No, silly, it's about relationships between men and women. I'll dig it out after dinner. You read it and then we'll talk."

Every idle moment for the next few days found Cole going back over Erin's strange reaction, and Mr. Bradley's lecture. Some things he'd read in the book his mom had given him seemed to make sense. Other parts were really boring. It was hard for him to focus for long periods. He kept envisioning the pictures and emotions of him and Erin kissing. The heavy breathing. Those butterflies in his stomach. The raging tingling sensation in his groin. He could feel her breasts pressed to his chest when they danced or kissed.

He shook his head. Maybe Mr. Bradley was right. Where would it end if they continued dating? But the thought of not being with Erin made his stomach knot up. Aside from the physical attraction, he liked her. He valued her as a friend and didn't want to give up seeing her. His stomach churned at the thought of not being with her. It's not just me though; maybe I should just wait and see what Erin thinks about it all. Tension eased from his muscles.

On Wednesday afternoon, as he stuffed books into his locker, he spotted Erin walking toward him. She stopped and gazed up at him. "Hi."

"Hi," he responded, dropping his head.

An awkward silence hung around them.

"Did my dad talk to you about us?" she finally said.

"Yeah. You too?"

"Oh, yeah. I was really mad at him, but Mom explained a lot."

"What do you think?"

"About us?"

"Yeah."

She took a deep breath. "I don't know, Cole. I really like you and all. But some of what they said makes sense. We've got a lot of time. I still want to hang out together, though."

"I do, too. It's all so confusing."

"Mom says we should date other people, but I'd still like it if you'd come see me now and then--even if you want to talk to Dad." She smiled.

Cole matched her smile. "We'll be friends then?"

"Yes, good friends." She reached up, wrapped her arms around his neck, and pecked him on the cheek.

~ * ~

Through that week and the next, Cole missed the beginning of his English class several times to lounge around the cafeteria during Jason's lunch period. He developed a habit of carrying a notebook and pen to jot down names of students close to Jason--some he knew, and some he didn't. This ploy resulted in little more than one page of names and descriptions, and him getting in trouble with his English teacher.

That Friday, Brockton won their final football game, ending the season with a nine and one record. According to the rankings in the paper, they were sure to be in the running for the state Division Five championship. They'd have to beat Ashville during the initial playoffs to make the semi-finals. Cole looked forward to getting revenge.

He chose to go straight home after the game and bypass the school dance. He couldn't quite handle seeing Erin dance with someone else. When he walked in his door, his mom and Mikey looked up from the left-over apple pie they were eating. They both jumped up and showered him with congratulations and hugs. "Man, your passes were bullets tonight, Cole."

"Thanks, Mikey" Cole rubbed his hand over Mikey's burred head.

His mom scooped a piece of pie for him while Cole poured a glass of milk.

"What do you want for your birthday dinner tomorrow, Cole?" she asked.

He looked up and swallowed the pie in his mouth. "What? You mean my birthday's tomorrow?" Cole held his eyes and mouth wide as he took a seat.

His mother reached across the table and gently smacked his head. "You don't fool me, young man. You know darn well it's tomorrow. You've been beside yourself trying to hurry it up so you can get your precious license."

Cole grinned. "Oh, that thing." He waved dismissively. "Yeah, I guess I'll have to get one, now that I'm sixteen." He shrugged.

She gave him a scowl and rolled her eyes. "So what do you want for your birthday dinner?"

He put a finger to his chin. "How about fried chicken, mashed potatoes, and those special green beans you make? Oh, yeah and cornbread... and gravy."

"Okay, and how about a cake?"

"Yeah!" Mikey shouted.

"Yeah," Cole mocked him, scuffling his hair.

"Tomorrow evening then. We'll celebrate in style, just the three of us."

Cole got up and gave her a hug. "Thanks, Mom."

In his room, checking over his homework, Cole reflected on his mother's and brother's attitudes. They weren't fooling him a bit. They were planning a party. He'd have to act surprised.

~ * ~

The next morning, just as he stepped from the shower, Cole heard the phone ring.

"Cole," his mother called, "it's for you."

He came from the bathroom with a towel wrapped around his waist, and took the phone.

"Hey, Bro," Dave's voice rang. "You got anything going today?"

"No, not 'til this evening, why?"

"Well, we have that science project due next week and maybe we can add some finishing touches to it. Plus," he crooned, "I just got the new Garth Brooks album; thought you might like to hear it."

"Garth Brooks? Man, you're a disgrace to your people."

Dave laughed. "I grew up on country, man. They are my people. Whaddaya say, can you come over for a while?"

"Sure. Soon as I get dressed, I'll head over to your place."

"Cool, dude. See ya."

Cole hung up and noticed both his mother and brother watching him. *They think they're so slick. Mom set up Dave's call. This will get me out of the house long enough for them and others to come to the surprise party.* He smiled.

He stayed at Dave's for lunch, then by late afternoon, headed home. Everything should be in place now--he'd given Mom and Mikey more than enough time. How many people would there be? There weren't any cars outside, no visible signs of a party, but of course they'd have planned it that way. He opened the door as nonchalantly as he could--and stopped short. No decorations. No people. No party. Huh?

Mikey came into the living room. "Mom had to go to the restaurant. She said to tell you she'd be back soon enough to make your dinner." He trudged back to his room.

Ah ha. She'll come trooping in with all my friends and yell surprise. Cole turned on the TV and settled in to watch the Ohio State football game. He reminded himself to stay cool and act surprised when they came in.

His mother returned--alone. She greeted the brothers before traipsing to the kitchen to start dinner. Cole sat, puzzled, on the couch.

After grace over the supper, his mother and brother each handed him a birthday card. While he opened an envelope, his mother placed a wrapped present in front of him. "Happy birthday, Cole. I'm so proud of the man you're becoming." She bent and kissed his cheek.

Cole rose and gave her a hug. "Thanks, Mom."

He tore open the wrapping and gazed at a shoe box with Nike Air Ultra Force stenciled on the top. He couldn't help the grin stretching his lips. He opened the top and smiled even broader when he saw the red and white gym shoes. "Perfect," he said. "Basketball season is just around the corner. I'll be the envy of all the kids." He turned and hugged his mother again. Mikey tossed him a small package haphazardly wrapped with more clear tape than paper. "I saved from my paper route," he said, with a smug look.

"Thanks, Mikey," Cole said as he unwrapped the package.

"It's a knife," Mikey announced before the present appeared.

"Wow," Cole exclaimed. "A lock blade Buck. That's so neat, Mikey."

After dinner, and a weak attempt at singing happy birthday, they dug into the cake.

Despite the disappointment, Cole lay content in his bed that night.

No party. Oh well. That's okay. Mom's been real busy lately and I bet money's a little tight too. Boy, those are great sneakers. Can't wait to wear them to school. Dave'll be so jealous.

~ * ~

The next morning during breakfast, Cole's mom said, "Maybe after church, we can take a drive. You need some practice on the freeway if you want to pass that test Monday."

"Wow, that'd be great."

"Can we go to Grandma's?" Mikey chimed in.

"I don't think so. Cole needs to practice on the interstate." She gave Mikey a look, before tossing Cole the keys to drive to church.

Cole exited the driver's side of the Fairlane when they arrived at church. He stood smiling in the parking lot, hoping someone would notice he'd been driving. Tomorrow I get my license, he wanted to announce.

After the service, Cole resumed his position in the driver's seat and drove toward the freeway. "Which way?" he asked before they reached the on-ramp.

"Doesn't matter. Why not go north toward Columbus. He drove across the bridge and turned on the left blinker. "Now stay in the right lane and drive slowly," his mom said.

"Okay, Mom." He gave a little eye roll that she luckily didn't see.

They cruised I-71 north until Cole spotted the off-ramp for the 270 bypass. When he braked a little late, he heard his mother suck in a breath. He entered 270 to drive east. "Check your mirrors," his mother advised.

Cole drove only to the next ramp and exited again. Then left across the bridge and onto the first ramp guiding him back to 270 west. He made an exaggerated dip of his head to see the outside mirror for his mother's benefit. She swiped her hand across the back of his head. When he reached the 71 interchange he turned south and headed home. Just before reaching the Brockton exit, Mikey's high pitched voice sang from the back seat, "Cole, look there's deer in that field."

"No, Mikey," his Mom's panicked voice rose. "Not while your brother's driving."

Cole wove the car easily along the side streets to their house. He parked the car in the garage and they headed inside.

"You did well, Cole. You should have no problem with the test tomorrow."

"Thank you." Cole took an exaggerated bow.

His mom grabbed Mikey and playfully swung him around as Cole led the way to the front door.

When he opened the door, a loud cheer greeted him. Noisemakers and shouts of happy birthday stunned him frozen in the doorway. He looked wide-eyed around the living room. Dave, Erin, several teammates, Mr. and Mrs. Bradley, Dave's mom and dad, even Mr. Bolton sat almost hidden by the crowd. His Grandma stood in the kitchen archway smiling.

"We got you good, didn't we, Cole?" Mikey pushed him further into the room.

He turned and tousled his brother's hair. "You sure did, kid." Mom stepped in and wrapped her arm around his waist. "Now, officially. Happy birthday."

"How'd you...? I should have known something was up."

Grandma walked into the room with a large cake afire with sixteen flickering candles. The crowd broke into a rousing rendition of Happy Birthday.

After cake and ice cream and more gifts, the crowd settled into groups. Some gathered around the TV to watch the Sunday game, others played board games, while the women mostly chatted in the kitchen. The doorbell rang.

"Would you get that, Cole?" his mom called from the kitchen.

He opened the door to a smiling Mr. and Mrs. Lutz. "Happy birthday, Cole," Mr. Lutz said.

Holding the door open for them, Cole said. "Thanks. Boy, this has been one surprise after another. Thank you for coming."

"We wouldn't have missed it for the world." Mrs. Lutz said.

"Mom's in the kitchen. Come on, I'll get you some cake and ice cream."

"Great," Mr. Lutz said, "but just a minute I want to show you something." He grabbed Cole's arm and tugged him to the picture window. He pulled the curtain back and motioned for Cole to look out.

Other than the neighbor's car across the street, the only vehicle Cole could see was Mr. Lutz's pick-up truck. Wonder where everybody parked? Seeing nothing else, Cole said, "What?"

"Look to your left, on down the street."

Cole leaned over to see farther. His eyes sprang open. A gleaming black sixty-five Mustang sat regally at the curb. Cole, mouth open and eyes wide, looked back at Mr. Lutz, who stood dangling a set of keys in front of Cole's face.

"Happy Birthday, Cole." Mr. Lutz grabbed Cole's hand and slapped the keys into his open palm.

"No Way!" It came out louder than he intended--and higher pitched, too. He took a deep breath to calm himself. "Mr. Lutz, I can't--just take that car. I mean... I've been saving for years to buy it. But I can't accept it as a gift."

"Oh, yes, you can. You'll need that money for insurance and maintenance on that old junker. Besides, at the rate you've been saving, I'd have to wait until you're twenty-one to get rid of that old thing."

Cole stared at Mr. Lutz's eyes. They glistened. Cole's heart sank. He knew Mr. Lutz loved that old car, and how much it meant to him. "I can't just take it. I'm not even sure I could have bought it from you. It was Jimmy's." Cole's eyes watered up and it became difficult to talk.

"I know, and he would want you to have it. It's not fair for such a loved car to sit molding in a barn. Sooner or later it'd turn into a pile of rust. You remind me a lot of Jimmy and maybe you can drive out to visit once in a while." Mrs. Lutz stepped over and wrapped her arms around Cole. "We'd sure like that, Cole."

Cole took a couple more deep breaths, looked back and forth from the keys to Mr. Lutz. "Well," he finally spit out, "you can forget what I said about baling hay for free next summer. Heck, I'll bale free for the rest of my life." His face broke into a huge smile.

"I wouldn't expect anything less," Mr. Lutz said.

Eighteen

Clutching the keys in his hand, Cole rushed out the door and sprinted to his car. He stopped short and stared at the Mustang. "Wow," he whispered.

Dave and Mikey skidded to a stop behind him. They, too, gawked at the gleaming jet black convertible. Cole moved in slow motion nearer the car. One hand reached out tentatively touching the canvas top, then slid down to the door handle. He opened the door and turned to Dave and Mikey. "Come on boys. We're going for a spin." He eased into the driver's seat and closed the door.

Dave and Mikey rushed around the car, jostling for the front seat. Dave won. A crowd watched from the front door and yard, as Cole started the car. He slipped the Hurst four-speed shifter into first gear and let out the clutch. The car bucked and stalled, rocking him and his passengers forward then back. He started the Mustang again and applied a bit more gas as he engaged the clutch. The car crept forward. Cole drove two hundred feet before pulling into his driveway. He turned off the ignition and expelled a deep breath as he sank back into the seat.

"That's it?" Mikey complained.

"'Fraid so," Cole replied. The birthday group gathered around the Mustang.

Mr. Bradley leaned down and motioned for Cole to roll down the window. "Did I just see you drive on a public street, without the proper operator's license, young man?"

"Jeez, I hope not." Cole responded, before displaying a huge grin.

Officer Bradley laughed, and shook his head. "Very nice machine, Cole."

Cole looked up at him. "It sure is."

"You'll need more practice to get used to that standard shift before you take your test, though."

"Yeah, but I'll get used to it. I learned to drive Grandma's tractor, so it shouldn't take long."

Mr. Lutz sidled up next to Bradley. "You gonna give him a ticket?"

Bradley tilted his head to Lutz and furrowed his brow. "No, of course not."

Cole gave a nervous laugh, wondering why Mr. Lutz would ask such a question.

"Whew," Mr. Lutz wiped his forehead. "Then I guess you didn't notice there's no license plates on the car either, so I guess I'm in the clear for driving it in here without tags." An impish grin stretched his mouth.

Bradley's brows shot up and his mouth hung open in a half smile. He slowly shook his head. "Good thing I'm here and not on patrol. I'd have called a tow truck to get it here." He clapped his hand on Lutz's shoulder and laughed.

He turned back to Cole as he eased out of the driver's seat. "If you need any help with the registration and title, let me know. I'm off tomorrow."

"That'd be great. Can we do it after school?"

"Sure. Come over to the house and I'll drive you to the BMV." He turned back to Mr. Lutz. "If you have the title, I can witness your signing. Like most officers, I'm a notary."

"Good," Lutz said. "Saves me another trip to town. Title's in the glove box."

As Mr. Lutz skirted around to the passenger side, the party group filtered back to the house.

Erin slipped her hand into Cole's and gave a gentle tug. He followed her away from the men. "That is the coolest car." She paused, her mouth turned into a pout. "But I'm not allowed in cars with anyone until I have my license. What a bummer. I'd love to go cruising with you."

"I could come over and park in your driveway. Maybe your dad would let us sit and listen to the radio."

"Yeah, I think that would be okay, but you can bet he'd be watching from the window, so no necking." Her smile warmed his heart.

~ * ~

By the next weekend, Cole had his driver's license, tags, and insurance for the Mustang. He tooled into Dave's driveway and tapped the horn a couple of times. Kitchen window curtains opened then fluttered back. Seconds later Dave burst through the front door.

He opened the passenger door and settled in. "You all legal, man?"

"Yep." Cole extracted his wallet and pointed to the new holographic driver's license.

"Cool. I'm right behind you. Get mine in the spring. Can't wait."

"You got time for a ride?" Cole asked.

"Sure. Where we going?"

Cole hesitated before making up his mind. Officer Bradley might get mad. But he knew he could trust Dave. "I've kinda been helping Bradley with a little problem lately. Now that I've got wheels, maybe I can do more."

"Huh? What're you talking about?"

"Okay," Cole sighed. "Mr. Bradley thinks there's some drug activity at school and Jason might be involved in it."

"What? Wow, that would explain some stuff. But what can you do?"

"Not much. He just asked me to keep my eyes open and see what I could learn. I tried following Jason a couple of times but he has a car and all I had was my bike..."

"Holy cow, why didn't you tell me?"

"Officer Bradley said not to tell anybody, but I know I can trust you, and two sets of eyes are better than one."

Dave stared ahead. Cole remained silent, letting him think it through. "Okay," Dave finally said, "What do we do now?"

Cole patted the steering wheel. "We can follow Jinks and see what we can find out about his activities."

"Let's do it. I'd love to throw that up in his ol' man's face."

"Would be sweet, wouldn't it? Pay back for your dad, and the coach."

As Cole shifted into reverse and backed out of the driveway, Dave sat silent--staring out the windshield.

Cole drove to a side street adjacent to Jason's street and parked where he had a good view of the gate entrance. He and Dave hunkered down to wait. Leaving the heater on would be more comfortable, but he didn't want the car exhaust giving them away, so he shut down the engine. "Don't know if he's home or not," Cole said.

"What are we watching for, man?"

Cole shrugged. "Whatever."

Several cars drove through the open gate during the next hour, but none were Jason's silver Toyota MR2.

"Not very exciting is it?" Dave said.

Cole sighed. "No. Maybe it'd be better to follow him when we know he'd be driving--like from school."

"And if he comes straight home? What's that tell us?"

"Not much," Cole conceded. His mood deflated. So much for Brockton Vice.

As darkness settled in, Cole drove back to Dave's house. "We'll try again but I need to think out a plan. This won't get us anywhere. You be thinking on it too, okay?"

Opening the door, Dave said, "You got it, Bro, but we're going to be a little busy with the state playoffs in two weeks."

"I know. Just think on it. We'll figure something out."

~ * ~

With no Friday dance and it being too late to call Erin, Cole sat bored on the family couch trying to formulate a better plan to spy on Jason. The late-night TV news droned in the background. Unable to think of anything new, he decided to just go to bed. The phone next to his elbow rang. "Hello," he said.

"Cole?"

He sat up fully alert. In that one word he had detected a pleading, in Erin's voice.

"What's wrong, Erin?"

"Oh, Cole. I need help."

"What's wrong, Erin?" he repeated, louder.

"I can't call Daddy. Can you come get me?"

"Where are you? Are you all right?" Cole's panic increased with her lack of immediate response.

"I... I don't know exactly."

"What do you mean, you don't know? Are you hurt?" he practically screamed.

"No... Not that, I mean I'm in some store."

"Where?"

"I don't know. It's a little carry-out. I think I saw a Speedway sign."

Cole's mind shifted to the only Speedway station in the area. "Okay, I know where it is. I'll call your dad."

"No!" she yelled into the phone. "Please don't. Can you just come and get me?"

"Yeah, but..."

"Please, Cole. I'll explain when you get here."

Nineteen

Cole drove to the Speedway station and stopped near the front walkway. He slid out of the car at the same time Erin appeared at the entrance. The heavy glass door caught her as she moved through, turning her sideways and away from him. She tripped, stepping off the curb and fought to regain her balance. He caught her before she fell.

"What in the world is going on, Erin?"

"Oh, Cole, I'm in so much trouble. Dad's going to kill me."

"Why? What happened?" He guided her to the passenger side of the Mustang and opened the door. After she sat, he ran around to the driver's side and hopped in beside her. "What happened, Erin?"

She put her face in her hands and whimpered. "I don't know..." She sank back in the seat and turned to him, face pinched and chin quivering. Red rimmed eyes told him she had been crying.

"I told Mom I was going to Holly's house to study..." She took a couple of deep breaths. "But we didn't. Janet Ingram, she's a senior, told us she and some other seniors were having a girl party at her house and me and Holly could come if we wanted to. Oh, I'll never be allowed out of the house." She buried her face in her hands again.

Cole listened, but couldn't understand all her distress. Sure it was late, but not late enough for her parents to get all bent out of shape. "But, Erin, what's so bad about going to a party?"

"You don't understand." Her shoulders slumped.

"Then tell me what happened."

She took another deep breath and let it out forcefully. "Okay, Janet said we were just going to make some popcorn and watch movies and maybe play some games. I thought her parents would be there, but then I found out they weren't and..." She heaved a sigh. "Well everything was going okay and some of us were doing that Twister game, and we drank pop and had brownies, and it was okay for a while. We were laughing and having fun."

"So what's the big deal?"

"After a while some boys came in and...Cole, they had beer and some other liquor. That's when I knew Janet's parents weren't home." Erin's voice sped up, "I started to worry. I was about to leave then, but when I got up, I felt dizzy. I thought it was from the Twister game, but the other girls were giggling at me. I laughed, too, but didn't know why." Her face pinched. "Then I heard one of the boys say, 'Did she eat the brownies?' Then I heard him say 'Good'. And I got real scared, cause it sounded evil. I couldn't seem to think straight. Then one of the guys grabbed me and tried to kiss me. I broke away and ran from the house. I left my coat there."

Cole's jaw tightened. "Who were the guys?"

Her eyes opened even wider. "I didn't know them... When I asked who made the brownies, Janet said that John had dropped them off earlier. Cole, I think there was something in those brownies. I felt so strange after a while. I still do. Then when that guy grabbed me, I panicked. I ran out of the house and just kept running until I found myself here. I still feel strange and dizzy. I just couldn't call Mom and Dad."

"Let's get you home. Your dad will know what to do."

"No!" Her hands shook and her eyes went wide. "I don't want to go home like this. Can't we just go to your house?"

Cole's brow furrowed. *What? This isn't like Erin.* He put his arm over her shoulder and pulled her close. "Erin, I don't know what's going on, but you have to go home. Your dad will figure it out."

She sucked in a few haltering breaths, before looking up at him. "He'll ground me forever."

Cole tilted his head back on the seat to think, and then sat back up. "Okay, you shouldn't have lied about the party, but this is something your dad needs to know about. You have to tell him."

She slammed her fists on the dashboard and glared at him. "You don't know anything. You don't know what it's like, having a cop for a dad." Her shoulders sagged. "No one wants to come to my house. They all make jokes about being arrested. I just wanted to have some fun, to be cool for once and now..." She looked at him. "You just don't know what it's like."

Cole stared back at her for a long moment, "No--but I know what it's like not to have a dad around. And I know yours. He'll understand."

"No, he won't. But I know I have to face him sooner or later."

"It'll be okay, you'll see." He put the car in gear and eased out of the Speedway lot.

Cole drove into the Bradley's driveway and went around to Erin's side to help her out. She leaned on him as they walked up the porch steps. The door burst open. "Where have you been, young lady? We've been worried sick."

She lurched to her dad and threw her arms around his waist. "Oh, Daddy, I'm so sorry."

Bradley looked past her and spotted Cole. His face went hard. Like a cobra, his right hand shot out and grabbed a fist full of Cole's shirt. "What the hell have you done?"

What the...? Cole's mind went numb.

Erin yelled, "No. He didn't..."

Bradley eased her away and pulled Cole to within inches of his face. "Boy, you know the rules. I can't believe you'd betray me like this."

The cold deadly squint in Mr. Bradley's eyes paralyzed Cole. The man's jaw muscles spasmed and a vein in his neck throbbed. Cole had never felt such immediate fear in his life.

"Daddy!" Erin screamed. "He didn't..."

Bradley pushed Cole back on the porch. "Get away from me before I do something we'll both regret."

The door slammed, leaving Cole standing frozen, wondering what had just happened. A booming voice echoed from inside the house.

Cole's feet somehow propelled him to his car. His hands shook and his stomach roiled during the drive home. The person he idolized wanted to kill him. Why? It's not fair.

He must think I kept Erin out so late--or something. The more Cole thought about it, the sicker he became. How could everything fall apart so quickly? Should he go back and explain? No. Mr. Bradley's too upset right now. Damn. He smacked the steering wheel.

Twenty

Late the next morning, Cole awoke to repeated calls from his mother to get up. After pulling on a pair of jeans, he stumbled into the kitchen bare-chested. He stopped short, frozen, as if he'd stumbled onto a Grizzly bear blocking his path. Fear pierced at his nerve ends. Officer Bradley sat at the table nursing a cup of coffee.

Their eyes met. Bradley held up a hand as a peace sign. "Sit down, Cole. I've got a lot of crow to eat."

Cole eyed the officer and warily sat down, scooting his chair back a bit.

"First off," Bradley said, "I'm really sorry for the way I treated you last night. Erin finally explained it all after I quit yelling at her. I hope you'll accept my apology."

Cole shifted his gaze from Mr. Bradley to his mom. She nodded. He turned back to Bradley, unable to form any words.

Bradley filled the gap. "I had the late crew pay a visit to Janet's house last night. But by the time they got there, everyone had gone and the place had been cleaned up. Her parents weren't home. But the girl is eighteen. There was little they could do."

Cole shook his head to clear the thoughts and images of what could have happened. "I didn't know what was going on last night. First Erin... Then you... you scared the crap out of me."

"I know, Cole. I'm sorry I jumped to the wrong conclusion." He paused. "Try to understand. Erin's my little girl and as a father I have to..." His face scrunched up as if he were about to cry.

Cole's mother put a supportive hand on Bradley's shoulder. Her face registered empathy for his emotional display. To Cole, she said, "You'll understand a lot more someday, honey, when you have children."

The old 'someday you'll understand.' Cole turned back to Mr. Bradley. "What was wrong with Erin last night?"

Bradley took a deep breath. "Near as I can figure out, someone must have laced the brownies with something. I took her to the hospital for some tests but the results aren't in yet."

Cole's eyes widened. "You mean drugs? Was it pot?"

"Don't know yet. Could have been pot but it could have been something else, too."

"Why would they put it in the brownies?"

"Fairly common. Especially if they didn't want the person to know. They had to know I'm Erin's father and who I am. So they might have been trying to discredit me. I just don't know yet."

"Who would want to do that and why?"

"Don't know yet. It was probably one of the boys. I'll get to the bottom of it eventually. In the meantime I just want to make sure you and I are okay."

"Sure," Cole waved a hand and forced a confident look, in an attempt to hide his remaining fears of what might have been. "No big deal," he said.

His mind whirled. Somebody tried to get Erin hooked on drugs or maybe one of the boys planned to rape her. Anger tensed his muscles. No more fun and games. Now it's personal.

"Okay then," Bradley drained the last of his coffee and rose to leave. "I've got work to do. And thanks, Cole, for bringing my little girl home safe and sound. I owe you one."

~ * ~

Monday, at school, Cole caught Erin at her locker. "Hi. How you doing?"

She hung her head. "I'm okay for a girl without a life."

Cole snickered. "That bad, huh?"

"Yeah. I think I'm grounded until I graduate." She grinned. "Hey, I'm really sorry I got you involved in my mess."

"No problem. You know you can call me any time. But I did think your dad was going to kill me. Man, I've never seen him mad before. I sure wouldn't want to be on his bad side for long."

"Tell me about it. He doesn't get angry often, but boy, when he does..."

After an uncomfortable lull, Cole said, "Erin, if you see any of the girls, or guys, who were at the party, would you point them out for me?"

A playful scowl appeared on her face. "You still trying to play junior detective?"

Cole felt his face flush. "N...n...no. I just want to know who to stay away from, that's all."

"Liar," she said. A smile brightened her face.

"Well... Maybe I can get some information that might help your dad find out who's bringing dope into our school."

Her face turned serious. "Cole, you'd better stay out of that."

"I can't." The first bell rang. "Don't forget to let me know if you recognize any of the guys who were at that party. Especially the one who grabbed you. See ya."

She sighed and cocked her head. "Okay."

~ * ~

Cole and Dave were finishing lunch in the cafeteria, when Erin approached their table.

"Hi, Erin," Dave called.

Cole turned to her as she bent to his ear. "Don't be obvious, but look to your right, over by the wash line. The redhead sitting on the far side is Janet Ingram. The two girls on either side of her were at the party too."

Cole snuck a peek, then turned and stared. "Holy Cow, I've seen her hanging around Jason Jinks," he whispered. "Was he at the party?"

"No. I don't think so--didn't see him. I would have told you."

Dave leaned across the table. "Yeah, I've seen her with Jason, too. I think they're a couple."

"Oh, the plot thins," Cole said, wiggling his brows at Dave. He turned back to Erin. "See any of the guys from the party today?"

"No, but the more I think about it, the more convinced I am. I've never seen any of them before. I think they might have been a little older. I would have remembered the one who grabbed me. He had a face like a monkey, and he smelled like a billy goat."

Cole and Dave rose with their trays. "Keep your eyes open and don't talk to anyone else about that party. If any of the girls ask what happened to you, just say you felt ill and went home."

"Why?"

Cole looked around, then whispered, "'Cause I don't want Jason to learn we might be wise to him."

"Okay, Cole."

~ * ~

After school, Cole and Dave sat hunkered down in the Mustang watching Jason's Silver MR2 on the other side of the parking lot. Jason appeared with the redhead attached to his arm. They got in the car and drove off.

Cole started the Mustang and followed, staying well back. Jason drove the town streets, winding his way to the north side. Cole thought he might be headed to his house, but he turned before getting to Walnut Street. Cole eased off the accelerator and coasted up to get a view. He watched Jason's car pull into a driveway in front of a large two story brick house. Cole quickly backed up and parked between two cars. He and Dave scooted down in their seats and waited. They had a good view of the MR2 through the trees surrounding the corner house on their left.

Jason and the girl sat in the car while the motor ran. After about ten minutes, the redhead left the car and headed up the walk toward the house. Jason backed out and retraced his route toward them. Cole and Dave slid down farther. Jason turned left and continued in the direction he had been driving.

"Whew. I thought he'd come our way and recognize your car," Dave said.

"Yeah," Cole said, easing the shift lever into first gear. "I'll have to stay further behind him, I guess."

Cole followed the MR2 long enough to see Jason drive onto his private street. "Not much sense in staking him out now. He'll have to eat supper and I don't want to sit here all night."

"I'll second that," Dave said. "I'm getting hungry already."

"At least we know there's a connection between Jason and the party. He has to be involved with the drugs. I wonder why they wanted Erin there?"

Dave thought a moment. "Maybe they thought she could help keep the cops away if she became involved."

"Could be. I'll have to fill Officer Bradley in," Cole said, as he drove past the gated street and headed toward Dave's house.

~ * ~

Later that night after dinner, Cole called the Bradley house. Erin answered. Cole hesitated when he heard her voice. "Uh... at the risk of making you mad at me again, is your dad there?"

She laughed. "After the other night, I'll never get mad at you again. Hang on, I'll get him."

"Hey, Cole," Bradley said. "How's it going? You planning to sue me for police brutality?"

Cole chuckled. "No, Sir, I just wanted to fill you in on what I've learned."

"What's that?"

"Well for starters, I think the girl who had the party is Jason Jinks' girlfriend."

"Really? I'll have to do some more checking on her. When I talked to her the other day, she said she didn't know any of the boys who came to the party. Said they just showed up and seemed harmless enough so she let them in."

"But," Cole broke in, "Erin said Janet knew the guy who brought the brownies. Said his name was John."

"Yes, I confronted Janet about that. She said one of the other guys told her his name, but not his last name."

"Did you ask her about Jinks?"

"No. I didn't know there was a connection at the time. I'll pay her another visit. Her parents spent the night with friends in Columbus and claimed not to know about the party. They said they'd deal with Janet for having a party in their absence. Didn't strike me as strong disciplinarians though."

Cole thought for a moment. "It doesn't make any sense that Janet would let strangers in the house. I wonder if Jinks was there and Erin just didn't see him. He's Janet's boyfriend. I'd think he would have brought the other guys with him."

"Could be. I'm sure Janet lied to me about not knowing the guys, and probably everything else too. None of the other girls knew any of the boys either. Or at least that's what they told me. Until I can get some tangible evidence of who's supplying the drugs, or I actually see some exchange, my hands are tied. There's a lot more involved here than just Marijuana, and I won't rest until I have somebody locked up."

"You said you had the night crew go to Janet's house that night. Didn't they find anything?"

"No. Several hours had passed and everything was cleaned up by the time they got there. They looked around pretty well without actually searching. I'm fairly sure most of the girls know Erin's dad is a cop, and when she left all upset like she did, they probably thought they'd better call off the party."

"It seems pretty stupid of them to invite her in the first place," Cole said.

"Yeah, I wondered about that too. In this small town, I'm sure they know of me. They're either stupid or trying some kind of set up."

"You think they might be trying to make you look bad, or get some favor or something?"

"Don't know, yet. We'll see."

"Any results yet of what was in the brownies?"

"No. The blood and urine sample had to go to Columbus PD's crime lab for analysis."

"Okay," Cole said, "well, I'll keep checking at school and see if I can learn anything else."

"Ah, Cole, I think maybe you should stay clear of this now. It's an official investigation and I don't want you in the middle of it."

"But I want to help..."

"I know Cole, but if you say something to the wrong people it might blow our chance to get any evidence. I'm afraid you could do more harm than good. And if this thing involves an organization, your life could be in danger too. I appreciate your help, but it's time to step aside and let the department do the investigation."

Cole winced. His wind couldn't have left his lungs any faster if Officer Bradley had punched him in the stomach. "I promise I won't say anything to anybody." The words rushed out like a frantic bull trying to throw its rider. "I can still keep my eyes and ears open and let you know what I hear, can't I?" Cole held the phone in a death grip.

Silence hung thick like a foreboding cloud. Finally, Bradley said. "Okay. But don't do anything except listen and watch. Okay?"

"Sure," Cole said, before Bradley could change his mind. "I'll let you know if I learn anything. Bye."

Twenty-one

Cole didn't tell Dave about Bradley's warning, so the next weekend when he called, Dave was more than willing to go on another stakeout. They sat in the Mustang, parked in their usual place, watching Jason's gated street. This would be their third attempt to track him. Neither held high expectations, but were excited about being undercover.

After chattering quietly for a while in the dim evening light, Dave said, "Why are we whispering?"

Cole whispered, "I don't know," and stifled a laugh.

A few minutes later, he jerked alert in his seat. "Pay dirt," he said, starting the Mustang. They watched the Silver MR2 pull through the gate and turn left on Walnut Street. Cole looked at his watch--seven-thirty. "He's finally on the move. About time."

"Probably just going to the store for his mom or over to Janet's," Dave said.

"Well, at least we get to actually follow him."

Cole had no difficulty staying well behind Jason in the small town. Not much traffic to blend into, but easy to keep track of from a distance. They drove through the business district and on to West Brockton, the less affluent section of town--familiar territory to Cole.

"What's he doing over here?" Dave asked.

"I'll bet he's either making a drug delivery or a pickup."

"You're obsessed with that drug stuff, aren't you?" Dave snickered.

"Well, why else would he be on this side of town?"

"Watch it," Dave said, as Jason whipped the Toyota to the curb in front of a run-down brick building with 'West End Bar' painted on the large window.

Cole jerked the wheel toward the sidewalk and parked well back from Jason's car. Even with cars parked in front of him, they had a clear view.

Jason disappeared through an adjoining doorway. Cole turned to Dave. "Probably goes up to the apartment above the bar." Cole pointed at the windows, lining the top of the building. "Boy, I wish we could follow him to see what's up there. Can you see an address on that bar?"

"No, but we know where it is. It ain't gonna move."

"Yeah." Cole sighed. I'm just trying to think of everything I can to help Officer Bradley later."

Dave shook his head and smiled.

About ten minutes later, Jason came out of the building followed by guy wearing jeans and a gray hooded sweatshirt.

"Can you tell who that is with Jason?" Dave asked.

"Nope. Not with the hood over his head."

The two suspects got in Jason's car and drove off. After a couple of turns they headed back downtown.

"I couldn't see any numbers on the bar," Dave said, as they drove by.

Cole followed at a safe distance. They drove back through downtown. The MR2 slowed on the bridge over the interstate and turned onto the northbound entrance ramp of I-71. "Where's he going now?" Cole said.

"Don't know," Dave said, "but don't lose him."

"I won't." Cole followed down the ramp. By the time he entered the freeway, two other cars had passed and were between him and Jason's car. Several times Cole had to change lanes and pass cars to keep up. "Man, I hope no troopers are around; Jason's going way over the speed limit."

After a while, the bright lights of Columbus showed on the horizon. "Maybe we should just turn around, Cole. We're getting a bit out of our territory."

"We will, but let's just see where he goes first. I've got a full tank of gas."

"Okay," Dave leaned back in his seat.

They drove past the glaring lights of downtown. After a few more miles, Cole caught the blinking right taillight of the Toyota. He slowed and worked his way into the right lane. They followed at a distance down the off-ramp and turned right on the surface street.

"Where are we?" Cole asked.

"Don't know." Dave shrugged his shoulders.

"Try to catch a street name when we pass an intersection."

Dave leaned forward for a better look out the windshield. At the next intersection, he said, "Got it. We're on Lane Avenue. Wait, oh crap, he's turning again."

Cole focused every sense on his driving. His forearms ached from gripping the steering wheel. The hectic city traffic posed problems he wasn't used to.

"Cole," Dave said, "this is Ohio State territory. That was High Street we just passed."

Cole focused on the silver car two vehicles in front of them. "He's turning again. Street name?"

After the turn, Dave said, "We're on River Road."

The street spanned four lanes with little congestion, Cole relaxed a bit. The next turn took them down a side street lined with older brick buildings standing practically side-by-side. Most of them appeared to be businesses and apartment structures.

"He's pulling over," Dave yelled.

Cole jammed on the brakes and pulled to the curb behind another parked car on the dimly lit street and turned off the headlights.

"I can't see what he's doing," Dave said.

"Driver's door's opening," Cole said.

Dave eased from the passenger seat to the dark sidewalk and crouched beside the Mustang. "The other guy is getting out, too."

"Looks like they're headed for the club across the street," Cole said.

The two figures crossed the street toward the neon lit bar. "Wait," Cole said. "They're not going in. They turned into the alley right next to the club. Get in."

When Dave closed the door, Cole eased the Mustang forward.

"Man, they'll see us," Dave said.

"Don't think so. I'll just drive by. See if you can spot anything in the alley."

As they cruised past the alley, Dave said, "There's a light about halfway down. Looks like they're headed there."

"A light? In an alley? You mean like a street light?"

"No, man. just a light. One of them on a pole over a door--with a metal shade over it."

Cole drove to the next corner and turned right. Another right at the next intersection took them back the direction they had come. About halfway down the block, Cole slowed.

"What you doing?" Dave asked.

"I saw an alley on this side of that street as we drove by. Should give us a clear view."

He turned into the narrow corridor and switched off his headlights. Lights and neon signs from the street ahead provided enough light for Cole to see down the empty alley. He rolled through the shadows, parked next to a tall brick building just short of the street, and shut the car off.

"Okay, in the glove box, there's a pad and pen. We need to make some notes." Cole focused on the light in the opposite alley, hanging over a recessed doorway. But Jason and the other guy were gone. Where'd they go? More than likely in the door. "Oh, yeah, there's a pair of binoculars in there too. Grab 'em."

Dave put the binoculars to his eyes. "Look," Cole said. "Somebody else is turning into the alley."

Three girls in the shortest mini-skirts Cole had ever seen strolled past the neon sign and turned into the side alley.

Dave zeroed in on the trio. "Wow."

The girls stopped under the door light and just stood there for a moment. When the door opened, light spilled into the alley. The trio entered and the door closed. Cole leaned back in his seat. "What was that?"

"Three hotties," Dave said. He put the binoculars back to his eyes and swiveled his head to the street. "More company coming."

Two more scantily clad females in spiked heels and mini-skirts walked toward the alley, their arms entwined in those of a tall black man wearing a shiny suit and a white, wide-brimmed panama hat.

"Now that's gotta be..."

"Whores," Dave finished. "Seen enough of them in movies."

The new arrivals also waited under the light until the door opened and they disappeared inside. For the next hour or so several more people turned and approached the mysterious door.

"Big party going on," Cole said.

"Yep."

"Can you see any numbers on the front door of that bar, Dave?"

Dave focused the binoculars. "Looks like 1122. The sign says it's the Flamingo Club."

Cole grabbed the pad and wrote the information down, along with descriptions of the people they watched enter the door. "That back door has to be connected to the club. It's the same building."

"But why are they going in that way? Why not just go into the club?"

Cole shrugged.

After a long stretch of silence and no street activity, Dave said, "It's a long drive home, Cole. That is, if we can even find our way."

Cole expelled a breath. "Yeah, I guess we're not going to learn anything useful anyway. And we sure can't just waltz in there." He pounded the steering wheel. "I suck at this." He sank into the seat, laid his head back, and closed his eyes.

"Hey, hey," Dave said. "Look what we got here."

Cole looked up. A lone figure lurched from under the light and bounced off the wall.

"That's Jason," Dave said, keeping the binoculars to his eyes. "Got him right in the light, and he's drunk as a skunk."

"Maybe he's high," Cole said.

Jason staggered across the alley and leaned both hands against the opposite wall, next to a large dumpster. The filtered rays of the door light silhouetted him as he threw up.

"Now what're we gonna do?" Cole said. "We can't let him drive in that condition. And if we do anything, he'll know we've been following him."

Dave sat silent, intent on the binoculars.

Cole jerked up farther in the seat. "I saw a phone booth at the corner when we turned. Maybe we should call the police."

"And tell them what?" Dave lowered the glasses from his eyes.

"Well, that there's a drug party going on in that alley."

Dave gave him a disgusted frown.

"Yeah, that wouldn't work, would it? We could at least give them a heads-up about Jason's condition."

"Hey," Dave said, putting the glasses back to his eyes. "Sombody else...Whoa! He just hit Jason and shoved him against the wall. I think it's the same guy he came with."

"What?" Cole swiveled his head back to the alley. Sure enough the second man, wearing a hoodie, pummeled Jason to the ground, and started kicking and stomping him.

Cole leapt from the car. "You get to the phone booth we saw and call the police. I'll help Jason." He raced toward the opposite alley. As he ran, he could hear Jason's garbled screams and grunts.

The man had his back to Cole, totally focused on kicking Jason. Cole sprinted on the balls of his feet. The guy looked up just as Cole drove a shoulder into his side, like blind-siding a quarterback. They both went down. Cole bounced up thinking the other guy would stay down. To his surprise the thug jumped up and squared off in a fighting stance.

They eyed each other a second, before the guy took a wild swing at Cole's head. Cole leaned back from the blow. He tried to see the face under the hoodie but the overhead light shone behind the stranger. Cole started to wade into the attacker when the guy reached in his pocket and pulled out a knife. The blade sprung from the handle. Cole stared at the weapon and stumbled back a few more paces. His own right hand dug into his pocket and closed on the lock-blade Buck. He pulled it out and fumbled to open the blade.

What am I doing? I can't get into a knife fight. I'll get killed. But he held it up for the other man to see. They circled each other. Cole's every nerve concentrated on his opponent. Fear gripped his stomach, as his brain screamed--Run! He skittered around defensively, trying to keep his distance from the attacker, and the silver blade he waved. Lurching to the side, Cole bumped into the dumpster and stumbled for balance.

An excruciating pain exploded in the back of his head. Next thing he knew he sprawled face down in the rubble. Multi-colored spots danced in his eyes. His brain refused to focus. Dizziness distorted everything. Shifting to his right side, he lifted a hand to the back of his head. It came away wet. Lying on the ground, Cole fought to remain conscious. He heard another voice behind him.

"Kill both the sons-a-bitches and let's get out of here."

A blurred pair of dirty sneakers approached Cole's head. He tried to push himself up but failed. The grubby sneakers straddled his head. Cole held his breath.

I'm going to die! His mind flashed: *Mom--Mikey--.* With his last ounce of strength, he lunged up and jammed his Buck knife to the hilt in the leg of the man standing over him. He heard his attacker scream. Cole tried to fight the dizziness. In the foggy distance, he heard, "Hey!" echo down the alley.

Then--a dark void.

Twenty-two

A sharp glare of white light speared into Cole's optic nerves, when he opened his eyes. He instinctively turned his face away and brought a hand up to block the intrusion. Was this the light everyone talked about leading the way to heaven? His head throbbed with every pulse of his heart. He moaned against the pain. There shouldn't be pain.

A loud screech sent renewed shivers of fear coursing through his nerves. Thoughts of a knife-wielding attacker flashed in his mind.

"Oh, thank God he's awake."

Somewhere in Cole's panic he thought he recognized his mother's voice. "Mom?"

Still blinded by the bright light, the room spun like a slow merry-go-round. He couldn't get his confused brain to work. He didn't recognize his own voice. Confusion morphed toward panic. Could he be dead? But he was blinking. Dead people can't do that.

A flurry of movement in his peripheral vision, and then a hand touched his forehead.

"Yes Cole, I'm here." She bent down and kissed his cheek. "You had us all so worried. The doctor said you might be in a coma."

"Coma?" He started to sit up, but the pain forced him back onto the pillow. "What happened?"

"You don't know?"

"Not really."

"Oh, no," she cried out. "He's got amnesia."

Cole's hands shot to his ears as new pain exploded inside his head.

"Let's wait for the doctors to determine that, Mrs. McKenna," a strong baritone voice said.

Cole's eyes slowly adjusted to the light. Deep breaths seemed to ease the pain in his head.

He tried to focus on the blurred face of hovering at his feet. "Mr. Bradley?"

"Had yourself quite a night, young man." A wide smile brightened Officer Bradley's face. "Had us all worried for a while. How you feeling?"

"Like sh... ah, heck."

Bradley snickered. "Cole, can you remember anything about last night? Dave told me you followed Jason."

"Last night?" Cole's brow furrowed, then his eyes opened wide. "Oh no, Dave--Jason..."

"They're okay. Tell me what you remember."

Cole sagged into the pillow and closed his eyes. "Okay." He opened his eyes and squinted in concentration. "Yeah, we followed Jason and another guy..." His face grimaced and he turned away. "Sorry."

Bradley nodded. One eyebrow rose with an I-told-you-so expression.

"We were in this alley in Columbus, watching a door Jason went in. He came out and puked, then some guy came out and started beating and kicking him..." Cole raised his head, then sank again into the pillow. "Oh, man. That guy kept kicking him. I thought he'd be dead for sure. I heard somebody say "kill him." Cole took a couple of breaths to calm himself.

Bradley pressed a hand to his shoulder. "Jason's alive. He's in recovery now. They operated on him early this morning. He has some internal injuries, but the docs think he'll be okay."

"But how did I get here? What happened? I thought he was going to kill me too."

On the other side of the bed, a black hand reached over the rail and clasped his. "You owe me big time, Bro."

"Huh?" he focused on Dave. "What happened, man?"

"I don't rightly know. I saw you down in that alley and screamed at the two guys, and they just ran off. They must have known how tough I am. Didn't want to take a chance, with only two of them against me." A satisfied smile lit his face.

Bradley play-smacked the back of Dave's head.

Cole took a deep breath. "One of them had a big switchblade, and the other one must have hit me from behind with something."

"Way your head's lumped up it must have been a baseball bat," Bradley said. "

"How'd I get here?"

"After I got to that phone booth and called 911, I ran back to the alley," Dave said. "Man, all that blood on your head. I thought you were dead, but then I saw you breathing. The cops showed up a few minutes later and then an ambulance. I followed them to the hospital in your car and called your mom."

"And your mother called me," Bradley said. "I thought I told you to stay out of this, Cole."

"I know." Cole closed his eyes and sighed. "But we didn't plan to do anything. Just followed Jason to see where he went. I couldn't just let him get beat up--or killed."

His mother bent and kissed his forehead.

"I filled the Columbus PD in on the details Dave told me," Bradley continued. "The investigating officer said he'd come back when you woke up to get a statement. In the meantime they'll be checking out that club. They said they'd keep me in the loop because it's tied to our town."

Cole tried to rise again. "Something bad's going on at that place..."

"I know. Dave told me and the detective about it and Columbus PD is investigating. Now don't you worry. It'll all get sorted out-- without your help." He tilted his head and scowled at Cole. "You got it?"

"Yes, Sir," Cole mumbled.

His mom put a hand on his shoulder. "You'd better listen to him this time, Cole."

"I will, Mom."

A nurse entered the room and shooed everyone away from the bed. She checked the monitoring machines hooked to Cole's body. "He's going to be all right. Now you all just go on home and come back tomorrow. I need to check his vitals and he needs rest."

"Can't they stay a little while?" Cole pleaded.

"No." She injected something into the IV tube dripping into his arm. "That's a sedative. Now you relax and get some rest. Best thing for healing."

~ * ~

Cole awoke when a nurse jostled the bed as she checked the monitor. The room lights were dim but his head still throbbed.

"How you feeling, honey?" the nurse asked.

Cole took a deep breath. "Okay, I guess. My head hurts."

"It'll go away in a minute or two. I just put some pain medicine in your IV."

Cole heard someone clear his throat.

A man rose from a chair and approached. "Is it all right to talk to him now?" he asked.

"Sure. His breakfast won't be here for a while yet." She eased away from the bed.

"Hi, Cole. I'm Detective Hill with Columbus PD. You feel up to giving me a statement?"

"Um... ah... Sure," Cole said, eyeing the stocky stranger. He wore a dark suit with a muted blue tie. The detective pulled a glasses case and a small notebook from his coat pocket.

"Okay then. Start from the beginning and tell me what happened."

Cole closed his eyes a moment. "We followed Jason Jinks from Brockton to Columbus yesterday evening..."

The detective interrupted, "You mean night before last, don't you?"

Cole's upper lip curled. "Two days? Have I slept that long?"

"'Fraid so, honey," the nurse called, as she opened the door to leave.

"Wow," Cole sighed. "Anyway, we followed Jason and another guy--"

"Know who the other guy is?"

"No. He wore a hooded sweatshirt and it was dark. He was the same guy beating up Jason though."

"How do you know that?"

"I don't know for sure but he had the same build and hoodie."

"Dave told me Jason picked the other guy up in Brockton. If he's from there wouldn't you maybe have seen him around town?"

"Yeah, maybe, but we never got a good look at him."

"Okay. Officer Bradley filled me in on why you were there." He scowled. "Not a wise move on your part, but I guess it was a good thing you were. Go on."

Cole relayed explicit details of everything he and Dave observed and his actions during the fight, ending with him being struck from behind. The detective took notes as Cole talked.

"How long was it between the time Jason went into the place and when he came out?"

"We didn't keep track but it was a long time. We were about to head home."

"And you thought he was drunk when he came out?"

"Yeah, we did... He staggered...but thinking back, he was kinda bent over holding his stomach. So I don't really know. He did puke, though."

"Did you see the guy who hit you?"

"No. It was dark and my attention stayed focused on the guy with the knife."

"Okay," the detective said, putting his notebook in his jacket pocket. "We have a felonious assault complaint on file for both you and Jason. We might change it to attempted murder." He tilted his head down. "You were lucky, young man. You could have been killed. I know you were trying to help Officer Bradley but this is police business. You stay out of it--understand?"

"Yes, Sir." Cole sagged into his pillow.

"We'll be in touch if we make an arrest." He turned to leave.

"Wait." Cole sat up. "What did you find at that club? I know something was going on there."

Detective Hill scowled at him, raised his brows and sighed. "Bradley warned me you'd be nosy and want details." He gave a wry smile. "I guess it won't hurt. The street officers raided the club right after the ambulance took you and Jason away. They made several arrests for drug possession and confiscated a stash stored under the bar. They arrested the manager for dealing drugs and operating without a liquor license, but couldn't locate the owner. Nobody seemed to know anything about the guys who attacked you. Or at least they weren't talking."

"But I know I stabbed one of the guys in the leg before I passed out. Didn't they find him?"

"Not yet."

"What about my knife? Did they find it? Their prints might be on it."

"No." Hill exhaled a sigh. He stared at Cole a moment with a scowl. "Okay... Yesterday we received a complaint from a local veterinarian who was held at gunpoint by two men who forced him to clean and sew up a leg wound. We think it's our guys from the club. He thought they were going to kill him. But he managed to escape out a back door when they told him to quiet the barking dogs. He gave a good description of the men and a white van parked in his parking lot. So we're on it. Don't worry, it's only a matter of time now. We'll get them."

"What about Jason?" Cole asked. "He must know the guy. He picked him up when he drove to the club."

"That's why I'm confident about getting them. We haven't questioned Jason yet. I think he'll be able to talk sometime today. Then I'll know more. In the meantime, you just rest and heal up. I'll be in touch when we need you to testify."

Cole's mind whirled. How lucky had he been? These guys are killers. But he couldn't stop thinking about ways to learn who they were. His mind was so occupied he didn't notice the detective leave the room.

Twenty-three

That evening, Cole lay bored out of his mind trying to read a book. He read the words but had no idea what the story was about. He glanced up when he caught movement in his peripheral vision. A smile spread as his mom, Mikey, and Dave entered the room.

"Boy, am I glad to see you guys. I've been going stir crazy in here."

"I'll buy the crazy part," Dave said. "How you doing?"

"I feel a lot better, almost no pain today."

"The doctor said there's no brain swelling," his mother said, "so you might be able to go home tomorrow."

"Tomorrow? Why not now?"

"Cole, you have a concussion," she said with a frown. "Things could still happen. We want to be sure."

His shoulders slumped. "Okay, Mom."

Mikey stepped close to the bed. "They said you stabbed a guy with your knife. Did you kill him?"

"Michael McKenna. That's a terrible thing to say. No, he didn't kill anybody and he only hurt him to save his own life."

"Geeze, Mom, I was just asking."

"Well, don't."

Cole grinned. "How you been getting along without me, little brother?"

"Good. I went through your room and looked in all your secret places." A devilish smile lit his face. "I found a Playboy magazine."

Cole tried to swat him but he moved away too quickly.

"Mikey!" his mom said, then focused her glare on Cole.

Dave snickered.

A soft knock at the door, saved Cole from her immediate wrath. They all turned as the door eased open. A man in a suit stuck his head inside. "Oh, I'm sorry. I didn't know you had company. I can come back later."

"It's all right," Cole said. "Are you the doctor?" He hoped he could talk him into an early exit from the boring hospital.

The man entered the room. "No." He hesitated. "I'm... ah... James Jinks, Jason's dad."

"Oh, ah... hi," Cole said.

After an awkward moment, Cole said, "This is my mother, and my brother, Mikey, and my friend Dave Thompson."

Mr. Jinks walked over and held his hand toward Mrs. McKenna, flushing when he looked at Dave. He quickly turned to Cole and said, "I just wanted to stop by and thank you for saving my son's life. You'll never know how grateful his mother and I are."

He walked to Dave and stuck out his hand. "And that goes for you, too, Dave." He hung his head a moment after Dave shook his hand. No one spoke.

"Look," Mr. Jinks began, "I've been a real horse's butt lately." He glanced back and forth between Dave and Cole. "Like most parents, I guess, I thought my son could do no wrong. I took his word for-- things..." he looked down, took a deep breath, and looked up. "Anyway, I owe you both an apology for my reactions. Jason finally told me... about the drugs and..." He shook his head. "His recent behavior. I'm so happy he's alive, I can't even be mad at him--yet."

"You mean he's awake now?" Cole sat up.

"Yes, and mostly out of danger--thanks to you two."

"Anyway," Mr. Jinks addressed Dave. "I can't begin to tell you how sorry I am for the trouble I've caused your family. I called your dad this morning and apologized. He'll be coming back to work on Monday."

"Wow, that's great," Dave said.

"And I called Mr. Stubbs and apologized to him for the trouble I caused Coach Wion."

"This must be very difficult for you, Mr. Jinks," Mrs. McKenna said.

"No. Not at all, Ma'am. Once the truth comes out, it's like a burden has been lifted. I didn't like myself very much while striking out at others." He looked at the floor. "But when one's child is threatened..."

"I understand completely," Mrs. McKenna said.

An awkward silence ended when Mr. Jinks said, "Well, I just wanted to thank you for doing what you did. If I can ever do anything to repay you just let me know."

"That's all right, Sir. I'm just glad Jason will be okay," Cole said.

"Me too," he said, shuffling toward the door. "Thanks again."

"Well, that was nice of him," Mrs. McKenna said, after the door swung closed.

"Yeah," Cole said. He turned to Dave. "We need to talk to Jason."

"No you don't, young man. You stay completely out of this from now on. Let the police handle it."

"Oh, Mom. We just want to know what happened. I won't do anything."

"I mean it, Cole. You'd better not."

~ * ~

The next morning when the nurse's aide came in to remove Cole's breakfast tray, he asked her if she could find out what room Jason Jinks was in. The morning nurse had told him the doctor wouldn't make rounds until after ten o'clock, so he had time to kill. A few minutes later, the aide returned and told him Jason was in room 232. She gave him directions to the room and left. No longer attached to the IV or monitor, and free to move about, Cole headed for Jason's room. He had a couple of hours until the doctor came and pronounced him fit to go home. Cole tried to act nonchalant walking the hall holding his gown closed at the back.

The door to Jason's room stood open. Cole poked his gauze-turbaned head in the doorway and rapped on the door frame. Jason's bed had been cranked up to almost sitting and a television game show droned. "Hi," Cole called.

Jason slowly turned his head and body. A hesitant smile appeared on his swollen lips. His face and body parts exposed from the covers were mostly purple. Cole walked to the bed. "Man, we look like we've just played the Packers without pads."

Jason grimaced when he started to laugh. "Yeah, I hurt all over. How about you?"

"Just my head, but it's not so bad now."

"I've got some broken ribs and my back feels busted but they say it's just muscle spasms. I think even my hair hurts. Pull up a chair, Cole."

Cole dragged a chair closer to the bed.

Jason clicked the TV off. "I don't know where to start, man. I mean, just saying thanks for saving my butt, ain't enough. You and Dave saved my life. And the way I've been acting..." He dropped his chin and turned away.

"Ah, I didn't really do much. Dave saved both our butts."

"Well, if you guys hadn't shown up when you did, I think they would have killed me. I still can't believe it."

"I know. Me either. But I'm glad we were there."

A silence hung a few seconds then Jason said, "Why were you there?"

Cole looked at the floor. "We... ah... Well, we followed you."

Jason wrinkled his brow but said nothing.

"Hey, I'm sorry man," Words spewed from Coles mouth in a rush. "but there's been some drugs coming around our school and somebody gave Erin something at Janet's party and she's your girlfriend and you've been acting weird and we thought you might be involved..." Cole paused. "So we followed you to see if we could get a lead on the drug suppliers." The plan sounded so stupid now, saying everything aloud.

They stared at each other until Jason finally said, "Well, you weren't far off. But I didn't know anything about what happened with Erin. I got mixed up with some bad people. I just didn't know how bad they were. I thought I'd just have a little fun getting high, and... acting all bad assed, I guess."

"Wow, man, I don't know how much fun you had but it almost got you killed."

"I know that--now. But I'm done with all that. I'll never do any kind of drugs again. I told that detective everything I knew about those people in Columbus."

"Good. I hope they can find the thugs. Do you know who they are?

"Only the one. He told me his name is John Smith--not sure I believe that. I've only known him a short while." Jason scanned the doorway and lowered his voice. "He's been getting the weed for me. He wanted to take me to a party that night and introduce me to some girls, and..." He glanced past Cole to the window. "Maybe some other drugs."

"Hey, man, you don't have to..."

"No it's all right. I've told my dad and the detective everything. I'm done with all that now, believe me."

Cole nodded. "What happened in that club? When we saw you come out, you looked drunk but you hadn't been in there long enough to drink that much."

Jason took a deep breath. "It wasn't booze, I only had two beers. I was a little high but not bad."

"What happened then?"

Jason took a deep breath. "Everything seemed okay for a while. There were some real foxes there and I danced with one. I really think they were hookers though, if you know what I mean. But then some younger girls were kinda dragged in through a back door. They weren't more than fifteen or sixteen, maybe younger. They looked pitiful and were stoned like zombies. There was a small stage and the guys took them up and made them dance a little. The crowd cheered and clapped and then the guys started tearing their clothes off and ... Jason took a couple of calming breaths.

"Didn't the girls scream or anything?"

"No they were too far gone. I saw tears on one of them. Anyway, the guys started having sex right there. And they forced the girls to..." He sighed and sank into the bed. "Man, it turned ugly in a hurry. They were gang-raping those poor girls and laughing and cheering. The whole crowd cheered, and then they started slapping and pinching them. I think they were videotaping it. The girls were really crying then."

Jason stared at the wall and shook his head. "I couldn't take anymore. I felt sick. I yelled for them to stop. Several guys in suits closed in around me and stared at me. They scared the crap out of me. While I was frozen looking at the guys in suits, somebody grabbed me from behind. John came up and punched me in the stomach. I twisted loose and ran for the door and when I got to the alley, I started puking. He must have followed me, 'cause while I was bent over, he knocked me down and began kicking me. I don't remember much after that." Jason offered a weak smile. "The police told me what you and Dave did."

"And you told all that to the detective?"

"Yep. And gave them descriptions and told them where Smith lives. They asked me a bunch of questions."

"Smith was the guy in the gray hoodie?"

"Yeah. How did you know?"

"Dave and I followed you, remember?"

"Oh, yeah."

"What else do you know about him?"

Jason closed his eyes in thought. "I know he's been in prison. He told me that. He once showed me some tattoos."

"What did you guys talk about while driving to Columbus? He say anything about where he came from, or where he worked, or anything?"

"No, not really. You know, just talk. You sound like that detective, man."

Cole grinned. "Sorry."

Jason's puffy eyes suddenly opened wider. "Hey, I think he might be from Brockton, but I've never seen him around town until just recently."

"What makes you think that?"

"Well, when we were driving down Ridge Avenue, he waved out the window and laughed. When I asked him why, he said, 'he was once arrested for stealing from that garden.' Can you imagine that? Arrested for stealing from a garden?"

Cole squinted one eye as the words sank in. He leapt from his chair. "Gotta go. See ya." He ran for the door.

Twenty-four

Back in his room, Cole scrambled in the cramped closet for the plastic bag containing his clothes. He found nothing. Mom must have taken them home to wash.

"What do you think you're doing, young man?"

Cole turned to the nurse standing at the foot of his bed with her head tilted down at him and a scowl on her face. He felt his own face flush. "Ah... looking for my clothes."

"Why? You're not going anywhere until the doctor releases you."

"But I have to go now."

"No way. The doctor will be here in a little while. Now you get your butt back in bed and wait."

Cole sighed and slumped onto the edge of his bed. He couldn't really leave anyway--he was stuck in Columbus without transportation. After a pause, he jerked up straight, and snatched the phone from its cradle. He dialed nine for an outside line then dialed his home number.

No answer. She must be on her way here or at work. He dialed Bradley's home phone. Mrs. Bradley's voice said, "Hello."

"Ah, hi, Mrs. Bradley. This is Cole. Is Mr. Bradley at home?"

"Hi Cole. No. He's at work."

"Shoot." He slapped his thigh with his free hand. "Uh, could you please tell him I have to see him right away?"

"Cole," she hesitated. "Aren't you in the hospital?"

"Yes, but I think I know who the dope dealer is."

"What?"

A momentary silence hung while Cole mentally debated whether to explain or not. "I'm sorry, Ma'am. Could you just tell Mr. Bradley to call me at the hospital? It's really important."

"I'll tell him as soon as he comes home, Cole."

"But I'll be home by then. Oh, ah, never mind. I'll call him later." Cole hung the phone and collapsed back onto his pillow.

A minute later he jerked upright again and grabbed the phone. He dialed his home number again and waited. No answer. Dang! He hung the phone and flopped back. She has to be working and Mikey's probably in school. He wasn't even sure what day it was. He briefly thought of calling her at work but decided not to.

The next two hours crept by at a frustrating slow speed. Cole paced the room, turned the TV on and off, and tried to read. Nothing helped. Finally the doctor came into the room and stood at the end of the bed reading the chart. He moved to the bedside and examined Cole's eyes with a pen light then took his pulse.

"Can I go home now?" Cole asked.

"I think so, later this afternoon. I'll call your mother and tell her."

Coles tightened his jaw. "She's not home."

The doctor grinned, obviously aware of Cole's anxiety. "I know. She left her work number for me."

"Oh yeah. Could you ask her to hurry, please?"

"I'll tell her you can go home today." He stared at Cole a moment. "Now listen, Cole," he slowed his speech, maintaining his stern look at his young patient, "you have to give your body a chance to heal. I want you to get as much bed rest as possible. You can go to school later this week, if you feel up to it. But not before at least one more day of rest, and no strenuous activity for at least a week. You got that?"

"Yes, Sir."

"Okay. I don't want to see you back in here any time soon."

The doctor left Cole fidgeting on his bed, his mind awhirl. He looked at the wall clock every few seconds until his lunch arrived. After he ate, he repeatedly walked from his bed to the window, staring down at the parking lot trying to spot his mom's car. He grew more impatient as the afternoon wore on.

Cole stood like a statue at the window staring at the inactive parking lot when his mother and brother walked into the room. His building anxiety caused him to jump when Mikey said, "Hi Cole." Obviously his vigil of the parking lot had been useless. How had they gotten by him?

He glanced at the wall clock. It was after four o'clock. "Where have you been all day?" Cole demanded. "I've been going stir crazy here."

"Young man." His mother's stern voice warned him to back off. "I have to work if we want to eat and I could hardly leave Mikey at home alone."

Cole hung his head. "Sorry, Mom. I've just been going nuts in here. I have to talk to Mr. Bradley right away."

"What about?"

"I'll explain on the way home. Can we please go now?"

She handed him a shopping bag containing clean clothes. He went into the bathroom and dressed.

~ * ~

In the car, Cole explained his deductions about the Shaw brothers to his mother. Mikey exclaimed, "Wow, I remember those guys from where we used to live. They're mean."

"Cole," his mother started, "you stay out of this from now on. Those boys are obviously dangerous. You could have been killed."

"I just want to tell Officer Bradley what I learned so he can arrest them."

"And that better be all you do. I mean it, Cole. You stay out of it."

Cole hung his head and took a deep breath. "Yes, Ma'am.

~ * ~

When the car stopped in the driveway alongside his Mustang, Cole flung open the door and sprinted to the house. The front door was locked. He fidgeted, waiting for his mother to arrive with the house key. Once inside he raced to the phone. When Officer Bradley worked day shift he got off at 4:00 p.m. He should be home by now.

Mrs. Bradley answered the phone. "Is Mr. Bradley home yet?" Cole said abruptly.

After a pause, Mrs. Bradley said, "Yes, Cole, but he's in the shower now."

"Could you get him, please? It's important."

Another pause. "No. But I'll have him call you when he's finished." Her voice registered her disapproval.

"Oh, sorry, Mrs. Bradley. I didn't mean to be so rude. Please have him call me at home when he can."

"I'm glad you're out of the hospital, Cole." Her voice softened.

"Yeah, me too. It's really important, Mrs. B. Tell him I have to talk to him."

"I will, Cole. Goodbye."

~ * ~

Cole poked at the supper his mother had hastily prepared. Bradley still hadn't called and Cole knew he couldn't call him again. When the doorbell rang, he jumped up and raced to the front door.

Officer Bradley stood on the porch with a grin plastered on his face. "What's up, Cole?"

"I know who the dope dealers are," Cole blurted out as he stepped aside so Bradley could enter.

"So do I. So what's up?"

Cole tucked his chin and lowered his brows as he leaned back. "You do? How'd you find out?"

"I'm a cop, remember?"

"Oh, yeah. Sorry. Have you arrested them yet?"

"Whoa. It's not as easy as that. These things take time. I'm working with Columbus P.D. and they're gathering evidence to take to the grand jury."

"But we know who they are and where they live--at least one of them. Let's just go get them."

"What do you mean, 'we' know where they live?"

"The Shaws--or one of them lives above that bar on McKaig." Cole put his hands on his hips wondering why Bradley didn't remember.

"The Shaws? What are you talking about, Cole? "

Cole couldn't get a handle on Bradley's statements. "Well, gee, what are you talking about? You said you know who the dealers are?"

Officer Bradley sighed. "As I said, I've been working with the Columbus P.D. and with all the information they've been able to gather, the main dealers are an organized drug distribution cartel in central Ohio. The intelligence leads to a financial investment group operating out of Columbus. The detectives also suspect the group is running a pyramid scheme to bilk money from investors, and a white slavery prostitution ring as well. But it will take a while to gather enough evidence to have them indicted. These things take a lot of time and work."

"Slavery?" Cole's face scrunched. "But what about the Shaw brothers?"

"Yeah, what about them?" Bradley had a confused look on his face that matched Cole's.

"They're the ones who attacked Jason and me. And they've been supplying the drugs to Jason. Didn't you know that?"

Bradley leaned forward and raised his brows. "What? What makes you think that?"

Cole paused to think. "Okay. I was talking to Jason at the hospital and he told me that on their way to Columbus, the guy who said his name was John Smith--the one in the hooded sweat shirt that I stabbed--told him that he was once arrested for stealing onions from a garden on Ridge Avenue."

"No?" Bradley said. "The same one you and Jack and Dale were..."

"Yep," Cole interrupted with a grin.

"I'll be damned." Bradley lifted his chin and squinted in thought. "I'll have to get my butt back to that hospital to talk to Jason about this."

"But I told you what he said. Can't you just go to where the one lives and get him? I think that one is Dale by the way."

"First off, we've been to that apartment and he's gone. The place was cleaned out. Not even a print could be found. Secondly, I can't use what you've told me as court evidence. It's hearsay. I have to get it straight from Jason."

Cole's shoulders slumped. "Now what do we do?"

"We--don't do anything... I'll," he pointed an extended thumb toward his chest, "check out Jason's story. The Columbus detective wouldn't have given any meaning to that statement about the garden, even if Jason had told him. You and I know what it means. Then we'll set about finding Dale and figure out who was with him on the night you were attacked."

"It was probably Jack."

"More than likely." Bradley's eyes lit up as a satisfied smile started. "If I can get those two, they might make a deal to testify against the cartel." He turned toward the door.

"Wait. I want to help find them."

Bradley turned back to Cole with a scowl. "No way, young man. This is police business and you've done all you can do. From now on you stay out of this."

"That's exactly what I told him." Cole's mom said from behind Cole. "And he'd better listen."

Bradley's face softened. "Other than getting yourself hurt, you've done a good job, Cole. This information is vital, but now we'll handle it. I'll keep you posted on any developments."

"But..." Cole started to protest until he saw the tilted head and hard eyes staring at him. His shoulders slumped. "Oh, okay," he sighed.

Twenty-five

Cole lay awake long into the night trying to remember everything he could about the Shaw brothers. His mind swirled back to the projects and his childhood. Where had they hung out? What did they do for fun, besides steal things? Who were their close friends?

Each probing question came up blank in his memory. He pounded his fist into the mattress. He'd grown up with them; why didn't he know more about them? Maybe if he went back to the projects he might find someone who knows something about them. He might be able to get some information that would help Bradley and still not be directly involved. Troubled sleep finally engulfed him.

Cole awoke and looked sleepily at the alarm clock. He sprang from the bed wondering why his mom hadn't rousted him. He soon remembered the doctor telling his mother he was to stay home from school at least another day. It was after nine o'clock, so Mom would be working and Mikey would be at school. Being stuck at home alone wouldn't be much better than the hospital. His thoughts about the Shaw brothers from last night resurfaced. Not much he could do about finding them now--or was there? After a short mental debate of the consequences, he dressed and went to the kitchen. He sat hunched over a bowl of Cheerios, still racking his brain about where they might be holed up. With the spoon halfway to his mouth he remembered the old abandoned warehouse where he had found the beer and cigarettes from the burglary of Bolton's store. The spoon fell into the bowl as he jumped from his chair and ran to retrieve his car keys from the wall hook. No harm in checking it out. He sprinted out the front door to his car.

Cole slowly drove the narrow streets of the housing complex being sure not to turn onto the street where Dale and Jack's parents lived. He knew that street was a dead end and didn't want to be spotted. Old memories flooded his thoughts--some good and some not so good. He didn't see anyone until he arrived at the community playground. There he saw only toddlers and a few young parents. He whacked his forehead with the heel of his hand. *It's a school day.* None of the older kids would be here until after school.

Exiting the projects, he turned right and headed for the abandoned warehouse two blocks away. He cruised around the block several times looking for anything out of the ordinary. No cars in the alley at the rear entrance. The building looked as abandoned as it had almost two years ago. A few more broken windows and more trash in the alley, but still obviously abandoned. He pulled to the curb and continued to scan the area. Finally he exited the car and walked cautiously down the alley to the rear door he knew led to a stairwell. His stomach tightened even though he was sure no one was about. He eased the partly open door wide enough to enter. The rusty door squeaked. His heart pounded in his chest and vibrated to his ears. The internal thumping seemed to drown out all other sounds. He stood frozen for a moment. Wearily he entered and crept up the familiar metal stairs.

With slow shuffling side steps, Cole inched down the second floor hallway with his back sliding along one wall. When he came to the first room, he quickly peeked around the doorless frame then jerked back. He peeked again. Nothing but dark shadows. He took a breath.

Should have brought a flashlight. The tense muscles in his back and neck along with his still pounding heart caused his head to ache. He leaned heavily into the wall and tried to relax. Why was he so tense? It was only Jack and Dale he looked for. But Dale had tried to kill him and Jack had probably been the one who told him to do it. This is different than a simple fist fight. Maybe he should leave this to the police. He shook that thought off. *They're not going to be here anyway.* He looked around for something he could use for a weapon.

Finding nothing, he continued his search. *They wouldn't be stupid enough to hole up here.* He relaxed, rolling his shoulders. When he peered into the next room, a blur of motion brought his heart into his throat. He stumbled back into the hallway, tripped on his own feet, and fell to the floor with a clatter that echoed in the hall. He saw a scruffy alley cat scampering down the hallway.

Cole felt a flush flood his face. *Scared of a cat. How will I ever be a cop?* He stood and continued down the hallway. The next room he checked was the room where he and Bradley had found the beer and cigarettes from the burglary. The same mattress lay on the floor next to the broken window. Trash still littered the floor. He had no way of knowing if it were new or old. He opened the door to the storage room where the beer had been hidden but could see nothing in the absolute darkness. Cole continued to search each room on the upper level until he came to another set of stairs leading down to the warehouse. This stairwell angled down along the outside wall then turned back to his left to empty into the old shipping area. Cole couldn't see beyond the landing below. He eased down the top flight. From atop the landing of the final tier of steps, Cole cautiously scanned the room. Nothing. By now satisfied that he'd failed to locate the Shaws, Cole ambled down the final stairs to head for the door on the opposite side of the large room.

When he stepped off the last step, Jack Shaw emerged from under the stairwell with a gun in his hand.

"Well, well, if it ain't Mckenna. Our old friend." Jack glanced toward the other side of the stairwell where Dale stood with a large kitchen knife in his hand. "Saves us the trouble of hunting him down, don't it Dale?"

"You bet," Dale said. His teeth were locked together and his jaw clinched. His lips pulled tight as if he were about to growl. He looked like a berserk lab monkey. Suddenly he made a lunge toward Cole jabbing the knife out. Cole jerked back toward Jack--and the gun.

"Hold it Dale," Jack ordered. "We got to figure what to do with him first."

"Sombitch stabbed me," Dale pleaded. "I'm gonna kill him."

Twenty-six

Officer Bradley talked to Jason Jinks at the Columbus hospital and verified every detail Cole had told him. When he left the hospital he went to the Columbus Police Department to talk with the detectives working the case. He related everything he knew about the Shaw brothers criminal records and the old onion caper. Bradley accompanied the detectives to the prosecutor's office and signed the affidavit for a warrant for the arrest of Jack and Dale Shaw for attempted murder and felonious assault. Bradley headed back to Brockton with a copy of the warrant. Based on the eyewitness accounts and the testimony of Jinks and Cole, he felt certain they would be convicted. Even more importantly, they might be convinced to provide information and testimony as to the kingpins of the drug cartel. They might plea bargain the charges down but it would be worth it. He had to find them first and worry about their involvement with the Columbus cartel later. Back in Brockton, he decided to call on Cole and fill him in on his day. He knew Cole was staying home from school today so he headed for his house.

He rang the doorbell and waited. When no one came, he knocked loudly on the door. Still no answer. He walked to the garage window and peered in. No car and none in the driveway. Bradley blew out a frustrated sigh. That boy won't listen to anything we tell him. Bradley headed for his cruiser.

He's probably out cruising the streets trying to locate the Shaws. I'd better find him before he finds some real trouble. Damned kid. This ain't a childhood game anymore. If anything more happens to him...

Bradley drove to the apartment above the bar where Dale had last lived under the name of John Smith. Cole's mustang was not in the vicinity. He checked the apartment--still vacant.

Bradley tried to think like a teenager. Where would he go? He made a U-turn and headed for the government housing projects. He stopped at Bolton's store.

"Hello, Officer Bradley." Mr. Bolton called when Bradley approached the counter.

"Hi Mr. Bolton. Have you seen Cole today?"

Mr. Bolton lowered his brows and tucked his chin. "No. Isn't he in school?

"Ah, no. He's out of school today."

"Oh, yeah, I read about him and the Jinks boy. How bad was he hurt?"

"Not too bad. Mild concussion."

"Why you looking for him?

Bradley didn't want to get into a lengthy explanation. "Just trying to locate him for some additional questions. He wasn't at home where he should be."

Mr. Bolton hesitated. He obviously had more questions but simply said, "I'll keep an eye out for him and tell him you're looking for him, if I see him."

"Thanks." Bradley turned to the door and headed for his cruiser.

Bradley eased his large frame back into the squad car. He sat in the parking lot thinking. His breaths came faster and he could feel his rapid heartbeats. He took a deep breath. The Shaws are probably long gone from this area anyway. It would be much easier for them to disappear in Columbus than here. Cole was probably in no danger. His nerves settled a little, he drove to the projects. He slowly cruised the narrow streets looking right and left for Cole's Mustang. Just as he was about to give up, he remembered the old warehouse. He stomped on the gas.

He spotted Cole's parked Mustang from half a block away. Something made the hair on his neck tingle. He jumped from the car and sprinted down the alley. He felt his heart thumping anew. He thrust open the rusted door and called, "Cole?"

No answer. *Should he call back-up?* Not yet, nothing to indicate any danger. He took the stairs two at a time to the top floor. Looking into the first room he cursed himself for not bringing his flashlight. Continuing down the hallway, Bradley checked each room but found no one.

~ * ~

In the warehouse dispatchers room on the ground floor, Dale's and Jack's heads both jerked toward the office door when they heard the metal alley door slam open, and a voice yell, "Cole."

"Shit," Jack exclaimed. "You watch him. I'll go check."

Cole sat on the floor with his back against a wall. His hands were tied behind his back. Dried blood streaked his face from a punch to the nose Dale had delivered. One eye was starting to swell and his lower lip burned from a bleeding crack. His head throbbed. He watched Jack ease out of the room into the warehouse, gun in hand. He headed toward the alley door to his left where the sound had come from. Dale stood over Cole with the knife at the ready. *He might kill me with Jack gone.*

Cole heard a rush of heavy footsteps on the metal stairs then a loud voice. "Stop! Police."

A shot rang out. Dale turned to the blast. Cole called on every ounce of strength and drove his leg up and between the widespread legs in front of him. A guttural groan and the knife clattered to the floor. Dale crumpled into a wheezing heap. Cole tugged his tied arms under his butt and managed to get his feet through so his hands were now in front of him. He sprang to his feet, picked up Dale's knife, and went for the office door.

Jack stood in the middle of the large barren room with his arm straight out and the gun pointed toward the stairwell. Cole ducked back inside. Officer Bradley's calm cold voice came from behind the stairs, "Jack, put the gun on the floor. I don't want to have to kill you, but if you don't put it down right now, I will."

Cole swiveled his head between Jack and Bradley. Jack hesitated.

"I mean it Jack. You had a clear shot at me before and you missed by a couple of yards. I don't miss. Now put the gun down--last warning."

Jack's shoulders slumped. He slowly bent over and placed the gun on the floor.

"Step to your left a few paces," Bradley ordered, "and put both hands on top of your head."

When Jack complied, Bradley emerged from under the stair well and walked toward Jack. Cole stepped out of the office as he walked by.

"I'll deal with you later, young man." Bradley's harsh voice slapped at him.

"Dale's in here, Sir," Cole squeaked out.

Bradley continued to Jack and handcuffed him. Leading Jack back to the office, he bent and picked up the revolver and tucked it into his duty belt.

"You okay, Cole?"

"Yeah, I guess so."

"You don't look so good."

He stepped around Cole, pulling Jack into the office with him. Dale still lay prostrate on the floor groaning. "What happened to him?"

"I guess I kind of kicked him."

Bradley shook his head as he stepped up to Cole and took the knife from his hands. After tucking it into his duty belt, he started untying he twine from around Cole's wrists. "Since I don't have an extra set of cuffs with me we can use this on Dale." He handed the twine to Cole. "Tie his hands behind his back."

Cole tied Dale's hands as Bradley had ordered. He cinched the twine extra tight around the wrists as a bit of pay-back. When he'd finished, Bradley said, "Let's go boys. I'll get the evidence crew out here to go over this place, but right now two of you are going to spend some time in the pokey." He turned to Cole. "Maybe all three of you."

Twenty-seven

The following Saturday the Brockton Broncos played in the first round of the Division Five state championship against their nemesis, Ashville. Cole hadn't been released by his doctor to play in the game. Frustrated to the point of practically giving himself an aneurism from screaming, Cole sat on the team bench with his head leaning on his hands. Alongside him Jason Jinks sat in equal frustration. Cole had convinced the coach to allow him and Jason to sit the bench during the game. Their teammates were taking a brutal beating. The freshman quarterback, Doug Gragg, had done the best he could with his limited experience and it wasn't all his fault. The rest of the team seemed to be playing in a fog as well.

The score stood at thirty-one to ten, with the clock about to run out. Ashville had the ball at the Brockton twenty-two yard line. To add even more embarrassment--twice--the Ashville quarterback took his knee at the snap, running the clock down in a sportsmanship gesture as to not run the score up. Thankfully the buzzer sounded, and amid the pandemonium from the Ashville fans, the Brockton team slunk sullenly to the locker room. Their bid for the state championship an embarrassing failure.

In the locker room, Coach Wion tried to ease their shame by congratulating them on their record and for making the state playoffs-

-his first as a coach. His words of encouragement didn't lighten the mood.

Dave finally stood among the bowed heads. "I may not have the right to say anything here but I'm gonna say it anyway." He spoke slowly and clearly. Some bowed heads slowly looked up. "Tonight..." he started, "we stunk as a football team, but Coach is right. We earned the right to be here. I don't know about you guys, but I'm going to remember this night. And I'm going to remember it fondly." He paused. "Yeah, fondly. Because I'm going to call on this memory during every practice next year. I'm going to use this memory to make me give all I can to ensure this doesn't happen again. We're a young team, guys, and we'll be better and stronger next year, so let's not let this loss cripple us. Let's make it work for us."

By the end of Dave's speech all heads were raised. Cole's chest swelled with pride for his friend. He started a slow rhythmic clapping that gradually spread through the locker room as the team joined him. A sly smile crept onto Coach Wion's face.

~ * ~

When Cole stepped off the team bus back at Brockton High, Erin stood in the cold night waiting. "Hi," she said when their eyes met.

"Hi, yourself. What're you doing here in the cold?"

"I heard your mom grounded you for at least one lifetime, with no driving privileges, so I thought I'd walk you home."

"Cool."

"Actually I'm only grounded until basketball season and that starts in a few weeks."

"It must be nice being a jock. Makes parents more lenient."

Cole pasted a wide superior grin on his face.

They started walking but neither spoke for a while. Finally Erin linked her arm with Cole's and said, "Cole, I've been wanting to talk to you but the time hasn't been right."

"What about? And what do you mean by the time hasn't been right?"

"Well you know. You were in the hospital and then that thing with Daddy and the Shaws and school and the football game and all." Daddy's real proud of you by the way," she rushed to get the last in.

Cole stopped and turned to her. "What's up, Erin?"

Her face scrunched. "I don't know, Cole. You remember that talk Daddy had with both of us... about us?"

"Sure. What about it?"

She took several deep breaths then blurted out, "Doug Gragg asked me to go to the movies with him."

Cole looked at her as she slowly turned her face up to his. Her eyes glistened. She looked miserable. He let a small smile creep to his lips. Then he gave a little laugh. "So what's your problem? He's a good guy."

"You're not mad at me?"

"Why should I be mad at you? You told him no, didn't you?"

Her face sagged and she mumbled, "No."

Cole laughed again. "I was only kidding. We both know we have to date others sooner or later. It's all right, Erin."

She heaved a deep breath. Then she squared her shoulders and squinted her eyes at him. "So why don't you care?"

Cole held her by both arms at her sides and focused his eyes on hers. "Erin, I like you a lot. I have very strong feelings for you. I wish we could go steady all the way through high school and college but I think we both know we can't. I don't like it but your dad is right. We have plenty of time." He paused, still looking deep into her eyes. "Will you promise to go to the senior prom with me?"

She smiled. "You silly. You'll be in love with somebody by then."

"I doubt it. Will you promise to go with me no matter who we might be dating by that time? That will bond us to be friends all that time no matter what."

She stared up at him. "Okay, you're on. But we can still go out together at other times too, can't we?"

"I sure hope so."

~ * ~

Coach Wion sat on a fold-out chair at the end of the bench nervously tapping his foot waiting for the whistle starting the first basketball game of the season. Despite his yearly success as a football coach, his basketball teams hadn't had a winning season in the previous three years.

The whistle blew and the referee lofted the ball in the air. Dave went high at center and smacked the ball to an open Brockton guard as everyone broke for position. From his forward position, Cole moved out to the foul line on the left side of the court. He took a pass from the guard bringing the ball down court. He dribbled to the middle and bounce-passed to Dave at the high post. Dave faked right then started a hook shot to his left. When the defender jumped to block it, Dave looped the hook under the defender and shovel-passed to Cole breaking behind him. Two steps and an easy lay-up got the game off to a good start for the Brockton Broncos.

The other team took the ball out and brought it down court. The Brockton zone prevented penetration, so the guard attempted a jump shot that missed. Dave went high to get the rebound. He handed the ball to the point guard next to him and sprinted for his post position. Again Cole came out of his corner when the Brockton guards could find no one open. Cole took the pass from Jason Jinks and dribbled to the top of the key as Jason broke for the basket, drawing a defender with him. Cole eye-signaled to Dave, who pivoted to his left to get under the net. Cole stopped and looped an alley-oop shot toward the backboard. As it descended its arc, Dave again jumped above the defenders. His hands snatched the ball from the air and in one fluid motion stuffed it through the net.

The roar from the crowd was deafening.

Sitting back down on his chair, Coach Wion beamed. His decision to start these two sophomores was beginning to look brilliant in the eyes of the fans. After all those losing seasons, he allowed himself to feel a little more confident in this year's team and the coming seasons.

~ * ~

Sergeant Bradley's cruiser sat nestled against the front bumper of Cole's Mustang in the school parking lot. Cole and Dave slowed their sprint as they neared the car. "Great game tonight, boys. Hop in the back a minute." Bradley said as they arrived.

"What's up, Officer Bradley?" Cole asked.

Bradley pointed to the new stripes on his uniform sleeve. "Not officer anymore boys.

"Wow," Cole said, "Sergeant. You'll be chief before we graduate."

Bradley chuckled. "Not likely. Anyway, I just wanted to show you that hard work and patience works. I also want to bring you up to date on the Columbus case. They finally wrapped up their investigation.

"Man, that sure took a long time," Cole said.

"That's kind of what else I wanted to talk to you about."

Bradley paused, looking around as if about to impart a secret. Most of the fans cars were gone. The few remaining fans drove slowly by the cruiser, trying not to stare. "Anyway," Bradley started, "I thought it was about time to have a serious talk with you. Now I don't know what your future plans are, Dave, but I know Cole has his mind set on becoming a police officer."

"Not me," Dave said. "I'm going to be a lawyer so I can make some real money."

"Good choice. So this is for Cole." He paused again to gather his thoughts. He turned to look at Cole. "I've watched you grow over several years and I guess I'll keep on until you graduate and leave Brockton."

"I'm not going to leave Brockton."

"Just listen. You might. Especially when you go off to college."

"Oh, yeah."

"So I want you to work on some things before you go rushing off."

"What things?" Cole cocked his head and knitted his brows.

"Cole, everything you did in helping with both cases against the Shaw boys, could have ended in disaster." His eyes bore into Cole's. "Sure, both times we got lucky and it worked out, but you put yourself in danger." He held up his hand when Cole started to protest. "I don't care what you think, you did. And it was all because of your impetuousness. Whenever you get an idea, you jump up and start running. You can't do that in police work. You have to bide your time, gather facts, gather evidence, and stay within the bounds of the law and department regulations. In short, you can't be a sprinter. You have to be a plodder and use your brain."

Cole hung his head. He knew what Sergeant Bradley said was true. Finally he spoke. "I'll work on trying to think before I act."

"That's exactly what I want you to do."

Cole nodded then said, "By the way, congratulations on the promotion. You deserve it."

"Not a better cop on the force," Dave added.

"Thanks, guys. Like I said you both helped out. I probably would have been promoted anyway but the help you guys provided sure didn't hurt." His smile radiated through the wire cage separating the front seat from the back.

What happened with the Columbus bad guys?" Cole said, anxious to change the subject.

Well, you know Jack and Dale made a plea bargain to get their sentences reduced in exchange for their information and testimony."

"Yeah, I sure hate to see them get off with a light sentence."

"Jack got three years so maybe he'll learn something from it."

"Probably not," Dave said, "and Dale will be out of detention in six months.

"Yeah, but I doubt either one of them will hang around this area after this," Bradley said.

"Anyway," he continued, "the Columbus detectives were very pleased with the information they provided. They used the contacts Jack and Dale gave them to get an undercover detective infiltrated into the organization. The undercover man compiled information and evidence until they had enough to go to the Grand Jury. Just the other day, the Grand Jury handed down four indictments against some very powerful business men in Columbus, along with the arrests of several major underlings in the cartel. They told me the evidence pointed to some major suppliers in Atlanta, Georgia, and the Grand Jury there is looking at the evidence.

"Wow," said Cole.

"Neat," Dave said.

When he finished, Bradley said, "By the way, I've nominated you both for a civilian citation for the help you provided in this case. If it goes through, they will notify you by mail. You'll probably have to come down to City Hall for a ceremony. You know how the mayor likes those things."

Cole and Dave turned to each other, nose to nose, eyes wide and mouths agape--speechless.

Epilogue

Twenty-two year old Cole McKenna's thoughts flitted to Tom Bradley as he sat at rigid attention in the hardback chair under the scrutiny of the Columbus Police Review Board. Cole had passed the written test, the physical fitness, and the psychological evaluation. This oral interview was the final step.

Five hard eyed veteran cops of varying ranks sat at a long table in front of Cole. "Now Mr. McKenna, can you tell this board why you think you want to be a police officer with our department?" the captain in charge said, while shuffling through a folder.

"Well, Sir," Cole began. "It's really been a goal of mine since I was fifteen or so."

"Why?" the steely eyed captain demanded.

"I was befriended by a police officer in my hometown about then, and I admired him so much that I wanted to be just like him, I guess. It's a little more complicated than that, but that's the main reason, and of course my degree is in Criminal Justice."

"That would be Chief of Police Tom Bradley," one of the other board members said, before retrieving a letter from the file in front of him. "He wrote this glowing letter of recommendation for you, is that correct?"

"Yes, Sir."

"The reason I ask," the first officer continued, "is that I just can't imagine why an apparently normal police officer, especially one of such high rank, would recommend a common criminal for a position with our department. That must be some hick town you're from, young man."

Cole's heart squeezed into his esophagus as he stared dumbfounded at the board members. His mind flitted to the burglary of Bolton's market, but left him confused. He had helped solve that crime, not been involved in it. Their investigators must have gotten some facts mixed up.

"Look," the Captain began. "You can't expect to become a police officer with a department like ours when you have a criminal record. How would it look if we hired every common thief from the street to become protectors of our citizens?"

"Thief?" Cole looked around helplessly. How could this be? His brain went into overdrive. They can't be serious. His lifelong dream shattered in a heartbeat. All those college years wasted on Pre-law and Criminal Justice courses. His shoulders slumped as he exhaled audibly. Something is wrong. They had to have wrong information.

Each face staring at him wore a cold, hard look. Cole sat frozen-- unable to breathe. The captain again looked at the file he held. "Yes thief. It's right here in this background investigation report. Apparently you were arrested--and convicted of stealing onions when you were twelve. Did you think we would overlook that?"

Cole thought he could detect anger building in the captain, but he couldn't figure out why. That childhood incident couldn't be such a big deal. His mind refused to function. His dream shattered. And he had no idea why. Maybe big city cops were different than those he grew up with. He and Bradley had laughed many times through the years of their friendship whenever the incident came up.

"But, Sir," Cole started to explain.

"No buts, young man," the captain admonished. Do you take this board for fools, coming in here wasting our time like this?"

Cole's astonishment and depression grew as the captain continued, "Perhaps you don't take this process seriously, but rest assured that we do. Our job is very serious. Do you know we sit in this room all day for weeks trying to weed out applicants who cannot match up to our standards? Do you know how serious that is? It's very serious. We have to eliminate all kinds of deviants applying for this job, and it's very serious. So serious," he paused and looked around at the other board members, "that we seldom get such a chance for a good laugh."

Roaring laughter filled the room. It rang in Cole's ears a moment, causing even more confusion. When his eyes registered the once solemn faces now smiling and laughing, he began to get the picture.

One of the members said, amid laughing, "Stealing onions. That's so good--a three dollar and fifty cent fine." The room erupted in increased laughter as Cole sat stunned and red faced.

Thus began Cole's indoctrination into the twisted sense of cop humor. Bradley had warned him.

Meet

Bill Weldy

William O. Weldy is a retired city police officer and retired high school teacher. He has written stories all his life, but only recently learned to write well. He now writes full time to try to make up ground